A SPLINTERED MIND

TRAGIC MERCY BOOK III

A Splintered Mind

Tragic Mercy Book III

E. A. Owen

Twisted Karma Publishing

A Splintered Mind: Tragic Mercy Book III
Copyright © 2020 by Twisted Karma Publishing.

Cover Design: Book Design Stars (Greece)

Author Website: eaowenbooks.com
Facebook.com/eaowenbooks
Instagram.com/eaowenbooks1

For My Children
Brooklynn & Phoenix

For Being My Biggest Cheerleaders.
You Mean the World to Me.
I Love You Always.

PROLOGUE

I don't remember much of my childhood. But what I do, I wish I could forget. My parents died in a tragic car accident when I was just three years old. Actually, a drunk driver killed them. The terrible part about it, the kid spent thirty months in prison for taking two lives—our parents. They weren't around for birthdays, holidays, graduations, weddings, or the birth of their grandchildren. They missed all of it, all the important stuff.

I apologize. I forgot to introduce myself. My name is Angel Walker. I am the youngest of four children: Mary, Michael, Matthew, and, of course, me. Our grandparents, William and Margaret, raised us in Astoria, South Dakota, a town so small, you would literally miss it if you blinked. The town, if you can even call it a town, is surrounded by cornfields and farmland. There are more cattle and hogs than people, which is perfectly fine with me.

Throughout the years, I have learned that people lie, manipulate, cheat, and steal. The world is a cruel place. A dog-eat-dog world. Everyone out for themselves. Very few genuinely good people are left in this world. Maybe I'm wrong, but what I'm about to tell you is from my experience, a life learned at a very young age that people you care about and love can be taken from you within an instant—no warning, no goodbyes, just taken and never to be seen or heard from again. Like I said before, this world is cruel, and you are about to find out more than you would probably like to. If you are fainthearted and have an unrealistic view of this world and think it's this beautiful, amazing place, this book is probably not for you. I will be blunt; I will be honest. This is my story.

PART I

First Memory

Gasping for air, I panic. My arms flail like a fish out of water as copious amounts of water that lap against my sunburned skin engulf me. Chlorine burns my eyes and nose as I swallow the toxic chemicals, and water fills my lungs. My heart hammers against my chest, the pressure building in my skull, screaming for oxygen. *Help! Someone ... Anyone ... Help me!* I desperately try to keep my head above water, but my legs and arms are weak. Lightheaded and dizzy, I fade into a black abyss.

***

I nearly drowned at the age of five. *That* is my first memory. The paralyzing fear tortured me for years. I'm terrified of water now. I never learned how to swim. My grandparents begged and pleaded, but I refused. I was teased and bullied—called a scaredy-cat and much worse. But it didn't matter. Anytime I would see water, my heart would race, and my breath would quicken. The anxiety was suffocating.

Being scared of water was just the beginning. I feared a lot of things, especially crickets and grasshoppers—really, any type of creepy crawly thing, especially ones that could jump. Just the thought made me shudder.

I remember lying in bed one night as a small child, trying to fall asleep, and that's when I heard it—chirping. My brothers and sister were sound asleep; my eyes were wide with fear. *What if it could jump on my bed?* Which was highly unlikely, since I slept on the top bunk. But my thoughts were anything but logic. *Eww ... What if it touched me, or even worse, what if it jumped inside my ear and crawled in my brain? What if I fell asleep and it jumped in my mouth or nose and thought it was nice and warm, made a bed and decided to stay there—forever?*

This is how my brain worked. I would overthink all the time. Overthinking always made matters worse. Of course, I never tried talking sense into myself; instead, I would drive myself crazy with all the irrational thoughts that infested my fragile mind.

My brother, Matthew, made it worse. He loved to scare the heck out of me. He would sneak up behind me all the time or hide and make creepy noises. One time, he scared me so bad I peed my pants. I was so embarrassed I locked myself in the bathroom for hours and wouldn't come out.

My sister, Mary, was always trying to comfort me, trying to tell me everything would be okay. She'd yell at Matthew to stop picking on me, but it never stopped him. He got a kick out of it. He said he would laugh so hard it made his stomach hurt.

My brother, Michael, on the other hand, was always getting into trouble. I swear he was in timeout most his childhood, and, when he got older, he would skip school and was always in detention. He got arrested a few times for petty stuff, but he was most definitely the black sheep of the family—the troublemaker.

And that leaves me, the scaredy-cat, afraid of everything, even my own shadow. I can't count how many times I would walk down our long driveway after the bus would drop us off, with Matthew and Michael running ahead, the big balls of energy they were, leaving me behind—alone, by myself. The wind was always howling, and leaves rolled across the gravel like tumbleweed. Frightened, I would hear something behind me, spotting something in the corner of my eye. Come to find out, more than not, it was just my shadow—how silly.

My grandparents did their best raising us, but they were much older. Matthew and Michael were a handful, entirely too much energy for their liking. "Settle down, boys," were my grandmother's famous words. She never raised her voice, not even once. She was as patient as they come—gentle, kind and was very generous with her kisses. She loved us dearly. She would do anything for us, but she became weak and started to forget things— simple things, things she had been doing for years. I remember once walking by the laundry room and hearing her crying.

"Grandma, what's wrong? Are you okay?" I must've startled her, because she jumped.

She turned around, forcing a smile. "Oh, sweetheart, I'm fine." She wiped a tear staining her wet cheek.

I frowned. "But you're crying."

"I know. It's nothing … I promise."

I didn't believe her.

***

Later that night after she had tucked us into bed, I heard my grandparents talking in the other room. I crawled from bed and tiptoed down the hallway to spy on them. I sat behind the corner wall to not be seen.

"I think I'm losing my mind, William."

"Why would you say such a thing?"

"Earlier today when I went into the laundry room, I stood in front of the washer for fifteen minutes, trying to figure out how to start the damn thing."

"But we've had that thing for years."

Grandma lowered her head. "I know."

"It'll be okay. You'll remember."

Grandma sighed. "I'm not sure. It's happening more frequently."

"Well, we're getting old, Margaret. It's bound to happen."

"But I don't want to forget. What if I forget you or the children? I couldn't live with myself." Grandma wept.

My grandfather wrapped his arms around her and kissed her forehead.

I slowly tiptoed to my bedroom and crawled up my bunkbed's ladder as Mary rolled over, grunting in her sleep.

GRANDMA

My grandmother gradually lost her memory. During the next few years, she got so bad my grandfather had to put her in a nursing home. He said it was the hardest decision he'd ever made. He cried himself to sleep every night for three months. I felt so sad for him. I wish I could say or do something to make things better.

But he was a soldier. Every morning, he would wake up and have our breakfast ready before we headed off to school with a smile on his face, trying to make the best of everything. But every night when we were all in bed and he was alone, he would cry. I don't think he knew I could hear him. There were so many nights I wanted to sneak into his bedroom and give him a big hug and tell him everything would be okay, just like he used to do with Grandma.

We had the same routine every day. We would visit Grandma after school for an hour, go home, eat supper, do our homework then spend the rest of the night either playing board or card games or reading books.

My grandparents were very adamant about family time. Before grandmother's mind slipped, she had taught me and Mary how to bake. Near the end, she would forget a step or two or burn the cupcakes. They tasted like cardboard. But, one time in particular, I remember the oven caught fire. Grandfather had to grab the fire extinguisher from the pantry to extinguish it. The oven was ruined, and they had to buy another one, but the smell of smoke and burnt food lingered for days.

Grandfather's mind was made up when she disappeared one night after supper. We searched high and low. He eventually found her on a deserted gravel road over a mile away, wandering in the dark and talking to herself. When he found her, she had no idea where she was or who he was. Her mind had crumbled right before his eyes.

Grandfather was never the same after that night. He changed. He was sad and lonely. They had been together for over fifty years and were high school sweethearts. Grandmother had told me they were inseparable since their first date. They had shared a chocolate sundae in a fancy glass with whipped cream drizzled in chocolate syrup and cherries, a wafer, and two spoons. And she knew from that day forward, they would spend the rest of their lives together—happily ever after.

But it wasn't all peaches and roses. They would soon learn the cruel intentions the world had in store for them. The endless tragedies that would make our family fall to their knees over and over again. It was as if God was playing a cruel joke on us. Just as we thought things were finally getting better, life made an abrupt turn and smashed head on into a cement wall, cracks spidering into thousands of disruptive veins, waiting for that last ping, and it would all come crashing down around us, like a treacherous volcanic eruption.

TORNADO

The stupid grin on my face, not even a scary clown could steal from me. My giggles filled the crisp autumn air, echoing for miles away. The crimson-colored lemon and tangerine leaves spun above me in the clear blue skies. The faster he spun me, the harder I laughed. My arms extended and legs kicked freely behind my body. My eyes darted as the distorted images circled around me, leaving streaks of color that looked like an abstract painting.

I was happy, truly happy. My dad's face glowed as my giggles echoed off the hundreds of big maple and oak trees surrounding our property. A small clearing overlooked Oak Lake. The trees were gigantic, and the reflections shimmered in the water below. The sun beat down on us, like molten lava, as the refreshing wind lapped my sunburned and freckled skin, sending shivers through my body.

The afternoons were hot and the nights cool—a perfect blend, reminding us summer was almost to an end and autumn was setting in. The sun was now below the tree line, and the sky was camouflaged in brilliant warm colors of magenta and tiger stripes, stretching its skeleton fingers and fading into the darkening sky.

The moon cast eerie shadows, and the streetlamp on the edge of our driveway buzzed and flickered. The dark clouds rolled in, and a low rumble echoed in the distance. The wind blustered, rustling the leaves on the trees. A flash of lightning violently ripped through the sky and touched down in a cornfield across the road, the corn stalks standing over eight feet tall.

"Dad?" I hollered, glancing behind me. Frantic, I checked every direction. "Dad!" My voice cracked. *This can't be happening. Not now.* A loud boom shook the ground beneath me, I gasped. Dreary, I blinked hard and tried to focus, realizing I was safe in my bed. I took a deep breath and exhaled.

It was just a dream.

A flash of light illuminated my dark room, and the rain pounded my window. *It's not rain, it's hail.* I was afraid to get close to the window, afraid it would break. I ran down the stairs to peak out the front door window facing south. The light hanging above the porch wasn't bright enough to penetrate the darkness beyond the security of the porch. The windchimes hanging on either edge of the porch whipped around ferociously in the wind. My eyes widened with fear when reality sunk in. *A tornado!*

I ran up the stairs in a panic and burst through Mary's bedroom door, screaming, "Tornado! Wake up!"

I rushed down the hallway to my brothers' room, tripping over my own feet but catching my balance before falling into the wall. "Wake up! Wake up! Get into the basement!"

My grandfather barreled from his room, yanked Michael from bed and threw him over his shoulder as we all scurried down the stairs. A window crashed to the floor, and glass scattered into hundreds of pieces. A big *thud* erupted behind me. A golf ball-sized chunk of ice fell just inches from my feet on the hardwood floor. The curtain on the window whipped in the wind. Our house was under attack. My heart hammered in my chest. I was terrified.

We safely reached the basement. Michael was crying. Mary stood frozen. I grabbed a hold of her hand.

Mary looked at me. "Are you okay?"

I nodded.

Michael paced back and forth. "How long do you think we'll be down here?"

Grandfather cleared his throat. "Until the storm passes."

We listened hopelessly to the tornado's fury as it destroyed everything in its path. The lights flickered, and more glass shattered. I'd never been so scared in my life. I squeezed Mary's hand.

"It'll be okay, Angel. We'll be okay." Mary forced a smile.

A few moments passed, and everything fell silent.

"Everyone stay here until I ensure it's safe to go up," Grandpa said.

***

He was gone for a long time. We all stood in silence, patiently waiting.

Matthew broke the silence. "How bad do you think it is?"

"I'm sure it's bad," Mary said as she surveyed the basement. "It sounded like we were under attack."

"Maybe the tornado took our house, like in *The Wizard of Oz*?" Matthew said, choking on his words. "What if we lost everything?"

"Everything will be okay. We still have each other," Mary replied, trying to stay calm.

"Grandpa has been gone a long time. Do you think he's okay? Do you think we should go find him?" Michael whimpered.

"No. He told us to stay here," Mary answered. "He'll be back. We just have to wait."

I glanced at Michael; he was sucking his thumb. He hadn't sucked his thumb in years. Matthew was biting his nails, something he always did when he was nervous, and Mary looked sad.

What if Matthew was right? What if we had lost everything?

Footsteps thumped loudly across the floor above us. Grandfather appeared shortly after with a frazzled expression. "I must warn you. It's a mess. Hard to tell all the damage outside, since it's too dark out, but I'm afraid it's bad. A lot of broken glass is on the floors, so please be careful."

I squeezed Mary's hand as we climbed the basement stairs, awaiting the dungeon of destruction. I just wanted to squeeze my eyes shut and pretend like it had never happened.

At times like this, it reminded me how much I missed my parents. I wished they were here. I wanted so badly to crawl in bed with Mom and Dad and let all my fears drift into the night. But they're gone. They're never coming back. I wiped away a tear.

THE AFTERMATH

A loud crash woke me from a sound sleep. Startled, I gasped as I flung upright in bed. The sunlight peeked through the curtain as I blinked my eyes open, wiping the sleepy seeds from my eyes. *My mom used to call them* sleepy seeds. I smiled at the thought and wondered what time it was.

I opened my creaky door. The silence in the house was eerie. I glanced in the boys' room; they were still fast asleep. Mary's door was shut.

I lightly knocked but no answer. I turned the doorknob and peered around the corner. Mary's bed was neatly made as always; she hated messy sheets. She was definitely the clean and tidy one of the family. I think she might have ODD or whatever they call it. I shook away the thought.

I noticed the window in the hallway above the staircase had been boarded up. *Must have been what woke me— Grandpa hammering away.*

"*Ouch!*" I grabbed a hold of my foot and cringed, yanking out a small shard of glass. The warm blood trickled down my foot. I grabbed a Band-Aid from the cabinet under the bathroom sink and slapped it on then slowly shuffled down the stairs, one step at a time.

"Good morning." Mary smiled as she tossed the debris from the dustpan into the trash.

"Good morning." I yawned.

"How did you sleep?"

"Okay, I guess. Where's Grandpa?"

"Outside."

I stepped onto the front porch and raised my hand, shielding my eyes from the sun. I gasped. The ground was littered with millions of fallen leaves, and golf ball-sized hail were scattered among the hundreds of fallen branches. I picked up one to examine it. The ball of ice sent a chill through my hand. I let it slide over my fingers as the water dripped onto the ground.

I stood in awe as I scanned the property. Trees had been ripped from the ground. Their long skeleton-like fingers, once protruding from the depths below, were now exposed and looked like spider webs covered in clumps of dirt. The grill that had once sat upright on the patio blocks out back had been thrown across the yard a few hundred feet away.

I heard a branch creak and spun around to see Grandpa's car stuck in our big maple tree. The massive branch bent under the weight then snapped, screaming in pain. I clasped my ears, eyes wide with fear as it crashed to the ground. Glass shattered, and steel bent violently upon impact.

A hand touched my shoulder. I turned my head. Grandpa's face was pale and his eyes sad. My heart ached for him. His legs wobbled, and he dropped to his knees. He covered his face with his hands and sobbed.

I stood there feeling as helpless as a miniscule ant. "Grandpa, it'll be okay." I wrapped my arms around him as tight as I could. My eyes were full of tears, and, when I blinked, the tears cascaded to the depths of my soul—drowning in despair.

THE PINKY PROMISE

It took us six long weeks before the ranch looked normal again. We spent every waking hour collecting sticks and glass and raking leaves, and we made several trips to the dump. Grandpa hired a crew of big men to put new windows, new siding, and a new roof on our house. When they were done, it looked brand-spanking new.

I spotted my brothers hiding behind a tree, giggling and whispering to one another, so I wandered toward them. "What are you two troublemakers scheming now?"

"Nothing." Matthew chuckled.

Michael leaned in and whispered into Matthew's ear again.

"What's with all the secrets?" I asked.

"Should we tell her?" Matthew asked.

"Naw, she'll be too scared." Michael smirked.

"Angel's a little cry baby. She couldn't handle it," Matthew mocked.

"Handle what?" I asked, curious.

"Don't even tell her. She's such a scaredy-cat," Matthew said.

"Am not," I pouted.

"Yes, you are. You're scared of your own shadow," Michael teased.

"Doesn't stop you from trying to scare me all the time."

"Of course not. It's funny. You're too easy."

The boys burst into laughter.

"It's not funny." I crossed my arms, pouting.

"Fine. We'll tell you. But you must keep it a secret. If Mary or Grandpa find out what we're up to, they'll put a stop to it straightaway."

"What is it?"

"Me and Michael took a walk into the woods the other day. We wandered off quite aways. We came across a creepy abandoned farmhouse deep in the woods."

"You did?" I gasped.

"Yeah. Looks like no one has lived there in years. The windows were boarded up, tall weeds growing everywhere. The porch is leaning and rotting away. I fell through one of the boards the other day. See." Matthew lifted his pant leg and turned his leg, exposing the deep scratch that stretched from his ankle to just below his knee.

"That looks bad." I cringed.

"Naw. It's nothing." Matthew shrugged.

"Whatcha planning on doing?" I asked.

"We think it's haunted," Michael replied in a creepy whisper.

"You do?" I asked, biting my nails.

"We want to sneak out in middle of the night and see if it's true." Michael glanced around us, probably to ensure Grandpa or Mary weren't in earshot.

"Why at night?" I asked, eyeing my feet as I kicked a rock. "Can't you go during the day? You can see better."

"That's no fun. Everyone knows ghosts come out at night, especially after midnight." Matthew's eyes lit up.

"That's kinda late don'tcha think?" I ask.

"Maybe. But it's our best shot," Michael said. "We want to know for sure if the place is haunted or not. You gonna come with?"

"Umm …" I focused on a bird that just flew overhead.

"That's what we thought," Matthew retorted.

"You're too much of a scaredy-cat anyways," Michael replied.

"Don't you dare tattle on us either," Matthew threatened.

"I won't."

"You promise?"

"Yeah."

Matthew extended his pinky. "Then pinky promise."

"Okay." I wrapped my pinky around his.

"It's done. She can't tell on us now," Matthew said proudly.

"What if she does?" Michael asked.

Matthew shook his head. "She won't."

"You can't know that for sure," Michael said, eyeing me suspiciously.

"Yeah I do. 'Cause, if she does … we'll sneak in her room in middle of the night and cut off all her hair. She'll look like a boy."

"You would not!" I grabbed hold of my long hair and pulled it to the front, running my fingers through it.

"If you break our pinky promise, I sure will," Matthew adds.

I harrumphed and frowned.

"When you break a pinky promise, anything is game." Michael smiled with a hint of evil lurking in the corners of his mouth.

"Nothing trumps a pinky promise, except a blood promise."

"What's that?" I asked.

"We cut the palms of our hands with a knife then press our hands together, and our blood seals the deal." Matthew smirked.

"I'm not doing that!"

"You better make her Matthew, or she'll tattle on us."

"I won't. I promise."

"Do you believe her, Michael?"

"I think she's too scared to talk."

"I think you're right."

My lip quivered. I turned and ran toward the house.

***

For the rest of the day, I had a horrible bellyache. It felt like my insides were twisting and turning, like an angry snake. I had a bad feeling about this. But then again, Matthew and Michael were right; I am a scaredy-cat. My mind raced, and I couldn't get it to slow down. It was giving me a headache. My stomach hurt; my head hurt; I was falling apart at the seams, all because my brothers wanted to sneak into an abandoned house super late at night and see if it's haunted. *How silly.*

But what if something happened? No one would know where they were. No one would hear their screams. It wasn't safe, but I couldn't tell Mary or Grandpa; I had pinky promised.

I flinched from a sharp pain in my fingers. I had chewed my nails to the quick; the skin was raw and throbbed.

I couldn't stop obsessing about Matthew and Michael sneaking out in middle of the night by themselves. Overthinking was causing my mind to go a little mad with these horrible thoughts. *What if a scary man is hiding in the woods, waiting for them? What if the house really is haunted and something bad happens, like the ghosts get mad and tries try to hurt them? What if they wander off and get lost?*

The thoughts were endless, and the more I worried, the crazier the thoughts became. *What if a rabid coyote is hungry and wants to eat them? What if a UFO zaps them into their spaceship and takes them away and we never find them? Bad things happen at night. Bad things happen when you keep secrets. Bad things happen when you sneak off in the middle of the night into the scary woods of dark shadows and creepy noises.*

My stomach continued to twist into knots.

The thoughts, endless.

SNEAK OUT

I tossed and turned, unable to fall asleep. I stared at the shadows dancing on my walls from the moonlight shining outside my bedroom window. The curtains swayed slightly from the breeze, and an owl hooted from a nearby tree while branches scratched neurotically at the window. They looked like boney witch fingers—long and skinny with gnarly nails. I pulled the blanket over my head and squeezed my eyes as tight as I could, wishing everything away.

I wonder what time it is. Have Matthew and Michael snuck out yet?

I crawled from bed and tiptoed to their room. I lightly tapped on the door and pushed it slowly open. The room was dark, and I couldn't tell if they were lying in bed or not.

A whisper escaped my lips, barely audible. "Michael." I whispered a little louder, "Matthew."

No response.

How long have they been gone?

I tiptoed down the stairs as the boards creaked under my feet. A bang from in the kitchen startled me. I flipped on the light and gasped at Grandfather sitting at the table in the dark.

He raised his head, squinting. "Angel, what are you doing up?"

"I can't sleep, and I'm thirsty. Just coming down for some water." I grabbed a glass from the cabinet. "Is everything okay, Grandpa?"

"Can't sleep either. Hard getting used to laying in an empty bed. Your grandmother and I shared the same bed for many, many years." He dropped his head, trying to hide his swelling eyes.

I turned on the sink facet. A scratching on the window in front of me made me jump.

"It's a windy one out there tonight," Grandpa grumbled.

"Sure is." I leaned over the sink to get a better look, but the light reflecting on the window made it impossible to see anything outside. Long skeleton fingers appeared, scratching at the window. Alarmed, I stepped backward.

"It's just a tree branch." Grandpa chuckled.

"I know." I gave a nervous smile then gulped half the water.

"Is something bothering you, sweetheart?" Grandfather motioned to the chair next to him.

"No, of course not," I replied defensively. I pulled out the chair and sat. I looked away, trying to hide my thoughts, even though I knew he couldn't hear the crazy thoughts chipping away at my nervous mind.

I pinky promised, I reminded myself.

"You seem awfully jumpy. Why can't you sleep?"

"No reason," I said quickly. I was never good at lying.

"Somethings going on in that brilliant brain of yours. I can tell," he said with a smile.

"Nothing. Really."

"Now come on, Angel. You can tell your grandpa."

"I can't."

"Why not?"

"I pinky promised."

"Pinky promised with who?"

"Matthew and Michael."

"What are those boys up to?"

"Nothing."

Grandfather stood, pushing out the chair with the back of his knees. "Those boys better be sleeping soundly in their beds."

"They are." I focused elsewhere as to not look Grandpa in the eyes.

"Mmm-hmm. I knew it."

"No, Grandpa. I promised."

"You didn't say anything. You never do. I can see it in your eyes."

I slouched and exhaled a big sigh.

"Where are they?"

I tensed up but didn't say a word.

"Now, Angel, you better tell me what those boys are up to or you'll get in as much trouble as them."

"But I didn't do anything."

"Keeping secrets is just as bad."

I shook my head.

"You better tell me, little girl!"

I frowned.

"We don't keep secrets in this house. Secrets are never good. It means you're hiding something."

"I didn't do nothing." I pouted.

The front door flung open and slammed shut.

I peeked around the corner to see Michael and Matthew standing frozen as a stiff board, their eyes wide with fear.

"Where have you been?" Grandpa demanded.

I quietly tiptoed up the stairs as to not be seen or heard. I got to the top when I realized I had been holding my breath. I lay flat on my tummy on the top step so I could spy.

"We-we-we were checking out an abandoned farmhouse," Michael stuttered.

"This late at night?" Grandfather asked, raising his voice.

Matthew stood silent, eyes staring, unblinking. The color drained from his face as he nervously chewed his fingernails.

"Looks like your brother has seen a ghost."

Michael snickered.

"Is there something you would like to share, Michael?" Grandfather folded his arms with a scowl.

Michael eyed his feet. "Um. No."

"You boys are in big trouble. I suggest you go to your room and get some sleep. It's late. We'll continue this conversation in the morning. In the meantime, you two better think long and hard about what you did tonight. There's going to be some serious consequences."

Matthew and Michael simultaneously looked at each other then at Grandpa then down at the floor, like they had rehearsed this a hundred times.

Grandfather pointed upstairs without saying another word.

Matthew and Michael glanced at each other then scurried for the stairs with their tail between their legs.

I shot to my feet and quickly headed for my bed. I crawled under the covers and pulled the blanket over my head. I laid there, listening to their footsteps and whispers as they passed my bedroom door. I was actually worried for them. I hadn't seen Grandpa this mad in a long time. But what worried me the most was that they would think I had broken my pinky promise.

THE ABANDONED FARMHOUSE

I hesitated with every step I took, my eyes darting in every direction. A rustle and snap from in the woods echoed around me. I spun around, breathing heavy, but no one was there. My heart hammered in my chest, and a bead of sweat trickled down my forehead. I walked in a trancelike state the rest of the way, as if someone or something was leading me there.

I finally approached the abandoned farmhouse deep in the woods, just like Matthew and Michael had said. I stood on the rotted porch, staring at the front door, afraid of what I would find. I took a deep breath and turned the doorknob, but, to my surprise, it was unlocked. The door creaked and groaned as I entered. I slowly manuevered through the maze of white cobwebs that had infested its surroundings, pushing them away with my trembling hand. I felt gross walking through the stench of mold and mildew that had permeated the walls of the creepy house of forgotteness, eyeing the thick layer of dust that suffocated everything it inhibited. Something wrapped around my right hand. I glanced down, noticing the cobweb clinging to my fingers, and I tried to shake it off in disgust. But the stubborn thing wouldn't let go, so I pulled it from the webs of my fingers and tossed it aside as it sent shivers down my spine.

Gross.

The floorboards creaked and moaned with every step, sending echoes of disturbance throughout the house. Just enough light escaped through the cracks of the boarded-up windows, casting eerie shadows onto the walls. With the light breeze outside, the dancing tree limbs made just enough movement to catch my attention, thinking something was in the room with me. Not that I already felt like someone or something was watching me and hiding in every dark corner of the room. This place gave me the creeps. I don't know what I was looking for, but something had drawn me here, like the house was calling my name. It wanted me to find something, but what, I was unsure of.

I stopped, holding my breath, and listened. But all I heard was silence. I wasn't sure if I had heard something or if my mind was playing tricks on me. Regardless, I needed to be careful. This house held many secrets, I could feel it.

It was tucked back deep in the woods. Whoever had built this place was hiding from something, or maybe I was overthinking? Maybe they just loved their privacy. But I saw no path leading to the house. If there was one many years ago, it had been overgrown by roots protruding from the forest ground, fallen leaves, and branches. The branches looked like skeleton fingers reaching out, ready to grab someone's ankles as they passed. The rocks and tree trunks surrounding the property were covered in a blanket of green fuzz.

A loud creak startled me. I spun around, but nothing but an invisible blanket of fear surrounded me. A picture hanging on the wall caught my eye. I wiped away the years of dust with a couple strokes. The dust made me sneeze. I watched as the dust particles floated away, trying to escape this unholy disaster. I leaned in closer for a better look. It was a charming farmhouse with lots of character. A mother, father, and three children—two boys and a girl—stood on the porch with serious expressions; no one was smiling. The black and white picture likened an old photo, maybe from the early 1900s. The house resembled this one from the outside, probably what it had looked like over one hundred years ago.

What a pity. This once-beautiful house was now a dump, falling apart at the seams and abandoned for many years. Neglected for even more. I stepped backward and surveyed the room for things that could have belonged to those unhappy children. What bothers me most about the photograph was none of them were smiling. They looked so serious. Why wouldn't they smile for the camera? My curiosity always got the best of me. So many questions but no one to answer them.

I heard a noise from one of the other rooms. *A whimper.* I followed the sound and came face to face with a closed door. I stood still, afraid what might be on the other side. After several seconds, I realized I'd been holding my breath. I let the air slowly escape from my lips, afraid to make the slightest sound. I took a deep breath through my nose and tried to muster any courage that could be buried deep inside me. I slowly pushed open the door, and it creaked loudly, shooting echoes that ricocheted off the walls. An electric current rushed through my veins. I took a step, then another as I scanned the room. That's when I noticed a little rocking chair in the corner, moving ever so slightly. My eyes widened in disbelief at a creepy doll staring back at me, taunting me. I heard a noise from inside the closet.

Startled, I gasped. A creature came busting through the door and lunged at me. I screamed.

***

Michael and Matthew rolled on the ground, bursting in laughter.

"I've never seen you so scared!" Michael shouted.

More laughter erupted.

"I think I peed my pants," Matthew said through laughing spells.

"I think I did too," I uttered, embarrassed. "You scared the living—" I paused, catching myself before I cursed. "Bejeebies out of me."

"What are you doing here anyway?" Michael asked.

"I was curious." I paused. "I was scared at first, but something drew me to this place. It's like I've been here before. I knew right where to go."

"Weird," Matthew said, standing now.

"You think?" I replied sarcastically.

"We heard someone come in, so we hid in the closet."

"We never thought it would be you. You're such a scaredy-cat. Thought it was Grandpa trying to spy on us after catching us last—"

"You broke our pinky promise," Matthew interrupted.

"No, I didn't."

"Then how did he find out?"

"He said he could see it in my eyes, that I was lying. Said I didn't have to say anything. He knew."

"That's bullshit!" Matthew scowled.

"I'm telling the truth."

"Do you believe her, Michael?"

"I don't know. Do you?"

Matthew peered deep into my eyes. "Hard to say."

"I didn't tell him anything, I swear."

"You think we should tell her?"

"No way!" Matthew thundered.

"Tell me what?"

"Sorry, Angel, but we can't now."

"Why not?" I asked with a frown.

"Because you can't even keep a pinky promise. That's why!" Michael shouted angrily.

"Fine." I folded my arms and turned to walk out of the room.

"Wait!" Matthew yelled.

I spun around, giving them both an I'm-not-impressed look.

"You tell Grandpa we were here and you'll have what's coming to you."

"Why would I do that? I'm here too, dummy," I said with a sneer.

SCARED TO DEATH

The next thing I remember, after that day in the woods, came years later. The reason I remember it so clearly is I have never seen Matthew or Michael so scared in my life.

***

"What happened?" I asked.

Matthew and Michael both looked at each other then back at me. The color drained from their faces, eyes wide with fear.

Matthew slowly shook his head from side to side—his eyes unblinking with what I surmised as *real* fear behind them.

"What is it? What happened?" I asked again, my voice trembling.

"If we tell you, Angel, you have to cross your heart, hope to die or stick a needle in your eye," Michael said with an uneasiness in his tone. It didn't even sound like him.

Something very weird is happening right now, and I'm not sure if I want to know.

"Please, Matthew. Michael. You're really starting to scare me. What happened? Please!"

Matthew, who had been standing as stiff as board, turned and walked up the stairs without saying a word. My heart was hammering in my chest now. Something was *very* wrong.

That's when I noticed the dirt covering his shoes, his pants, his forearms, and under his fingernails. Michael trembled, and his eyes had turned to glass. I swallowed hard. A horrible chill passed through me. I stepped backward; my lips parted in shock.

His eyes rolled in the back of his head, and he fell to the floor with a *thud*.

I rushed to him and kneeled over his body and shook him. "Michael. Wake up!" I pressed my hand to his forehead as the heat radiated through me. *Holy shit!* Taking quick breaths, my gaze darted around the room. I didn't know what to do; I panicked. "Grandpa!" I hollered, trying to yell loud enough for him to hear me outside. "*Grandpa!*"

It's no use. He can't hear me.

I stood and left Michael's unconscious body as I ran outside. "Grandpa!" I scanned the property, but he was nowhere in sight. I ran around the back of the house. "Grandpa!" I ran back inside, picked up the phone and dialed 9-1-1.

***

Matthew and Michael refused to discuss it. Whatever it was, it had scared the shit out of them. But it explained a lot. I didn't understand it, but, if what they said was true, I didn't want any part of it. I wanted it as far from here as possible. I didn't believe in ghosts or the paranormal, but what happened that day was anything far from normal.

Mary had visited to tell us she had met the guy of her dreams; she was pregnant and getting married. The boys gave her something of Mom's they had found in the attic—an antique box. They said it gave them the creeps, and they wanted it out of the house.

Of course, Mary, the calm and responsible one of the bunch, reassured them it was just a box and she'd love to take it, especially since it was our mother's. And since we didn't have much of anything of our parents' belongings— they had disposed of most of it when they had moved to South Dakota—she would keep it in a safe place.

After that night, the night Michael had fainted, it was pretty quiet in our house. It wasn't long after when Grandma passed away in her sleep at the nursing home. Grandpa was devastated. He didn't last much longer. I had always heard that older couples who had been together for a very long time died usually within the same year of each other, like one can't live without the other. True love.

Even though Grandma was in the nursing home for a few years with Alzheimer's—we had visited her almost every day—and even though she didn't remember us, it was difficult to see her like that, but it was even harder on Grandpa. It was like he had lost a part of himself that day. I hated hearing him cry himself to sleep after we went to bed at night. I felt terrible for Grandpa. I wanted to hug him and make everything better.

Matthew and Michael didn't make things any easier. Grandpa used to always say, "Boys will be boys." And he was right. They were troublemakers, especially Michael— always skipping school and getting detention. Then, when he got older, he got arrested a few times and spent a couple nights in the clinker—as Matthew would call it.

I supposed that was what happened when you lose everyone close to you at a young age. First our parents, then our grandparents.

Girls will cry, and boys will act out. That was how we dealt with our emotions.

***

After Mary got married and our grandparents passed away, Matthew decided to man up and support me and Michael. He didn't want us going into foster homes. Mary offered, but she had a baby of her own; she didn't need us disrupting her new life. At least that's what Matthew had said. Besides, Mary said Mom and Dad had big life insurance policies, and our grandparents had put it in a trust fund for us until we turned eighteen. She said there was enough money that none of us would have to work for a very long time if we didn't want to.

Matthew was seventeen, Michael was sixteen, and I was eleven. With a few connections, Mary's husband Elliott could get Matthew's trust fund released a year early.

Matthew really stepped up to the plate. He had seemed to mature into a responsible young man overnight. It was his senior year, and he worked a part-time job at the grocery store, stocking shelves. With his portion of the insurance money, he paid off Mom and Dad's house and bought a new BMW. He was living the dream.

Matthew made sure me and Michael were taken care of—food in the fridge, clean clothes, and cooked meals. He struggled with the cooking, but he knew the basics, and that was enough for us to get by. And, of course, I helped with the cleaning. I actually liked to clean. I wasn't nearly as organized and tidy as Mary, but I was only eleven. But we managed as three kids with minimal adult supervision.

After the cops arrested Michael for petty theft and he landed himself in jail again, Mary took me under her wing. I helped her with the baby, helped clean the house, and other chores. She wanted to step in sooner, but Matthew was adamant about being able to take care of us. She wanted to give him the benefit of the doubt but kept a close eye on us, checking on us often either over the phone or in person.

***

I lived with Mary for six years before attending college. Once I turned eighteen, I bought a little house in town. A sign reading, *Astoria Next 4 Exits*, sat at the Astoria border. It was joke of course—four exits equals four streets. It seemed like everyone knew each other, which could be a good or bad thing. I hadn't decided yet.

I was so proud of my house, a place to call my own. The two-story Victorian home featured dark charcoal-gray paint and white decorative trim. Small towers with complicated, asymmetrical shapes and a massive front porch accentuated the front. Beautiful vibrant flowers—tiger lilies and day lilies, tulips and amaryllis—surrounded the foundation. A two-car garage and a large shed sat on more than an acre of property. The best part was that it was on the edge of town, tucked away in a corner with plenty of privacy and big maple trees.

The charming interior boasted mahogany hardwood floors and trim, vaulted ceilings, stunning chandeliers, and a curved staircase leading to a balcony overlooking the main floor. I felt like a queen. It was definitely too big for one person, but I loved it, and it was all mine.

I would soon realize money was a magnet to the most selfish, greedy people who sucked others dry and drained every last drop from one's soul. They were the scum of the earth who lurk at the bottom of the ocean, waiting for its prey. They'd wait until an unsuspecting person were at their lowest, most desperate times, then they would chew them up and spit them out.

I was about to find a man who would turn my entire world upside down and a friend who would come to the rescue.

JAKE

What wasn't appealing? I was young, attractive, and, of course, loaded. But I'd give it all away just to have my parents back. But I don't get to make that choice. So, I must deal with the terrible aftermath of being tragically broken. My heart had been shattered into a thousand pieces and sewn up nice and pretty, hiding the imperfections and flaws that death and life had bestowed upon my delicate soul.

I tried to be happy, I truly did. But life did that sometimes. It could rip everything right from underneath, and I would fall face first into the ground, bloody nose and all. But I always got up, brushed myself off and tried again.

I was a fighter. I was stubborn. I wouldn't give up. And, when I felt down and started feeling sorry for myself, I would drown myself in music or bury myself in a good book—a way to escape reality without any toxic drugs or alcohol blurring my vision. I never understood how people could intentionally put something dangerous and harmful into their body, hoping it would make themselves feel better. An oxymoron, really. True, it might temporarily make them feel better, but, in the long run, they'd slowly deteriorate, causing more pain and suffering.

I hardly remembered my parents. To be honest, I didn't think I'd remember them at all. I was too young. The photographs over time would confuse me, and I'd start mistaking them for memories.

Mary and my grandmother would tell me how I was a miracle baby. My mom had serious complications after she had miscarried. The doctor had said she couldn't have any more children. But, a year later, she had found out she was pregnant with me. She had been skeptical at first, and scared, as anyone would under the circumstances, but I was a healthy little girl. They had decided to name me, Angelina Hope Walker, their *Angel of Hope*.

So, of course, you understand, I was born with high expectations, and I wasn't about to take the easy road. My life had purpose. I was born for a reason, and I wasn't about to let it go to waste. I would make the best of it, even with all the catastrophes along the way.

I was determined.

And then I met Jake. He was tall, handsome, charming, and confident, with a magnetic personality. His eyes were ice blue, and his features were strong. He stood at 6'4", 220lbs, with a square jaw, oval-shaped face, and a buzz cut. He had a warm, inviting smile that made my heart drool.

I should've seen the warning signs. I should've been more cautious. I should've never let down my guard. But I did.

The walls I had built didn't just crumble, they came crashing down. One day, I was single, and the next, my brain was a thick fog disguised as fluffy clouds with rainbows, butterflies, and glitter swimming around.

I met Jake at the grocery store. He was busy talking on his phone when I was leaving the store with a few bags. We collided. It was messy. A dozen eggs in one of the bags broke.

"I am so sorry. Are you okay?" he asked then whispered into his phone, "I have to let you go. Talk to you later." He shoved his phone in his back pocket and collected the few items that had rolled across the parking lot.

When he stood up, our eyes met, and we held the gaze for a while. He made my heart skip a beat. I know it sounds cliché, but I can't describe it any other way. He was dreamy. He was …. I swallowed hard. *Perfect.*

"Um … yeah," I replied, shaking away the thoughts. I felt my cheeks burn bright red and looked away.

"I didn't realize you cooked on the first date," he said with a smirk.

"Huh?" I mumbled, confused.

"The scrambled eggs …" He pointed to the ground.

"Oh, yeah." I chuckled with embarrassment. "Maybe next time I'll learn how to cook them."

"Next time, it is." He smiled, showing his straight, pearly white teeth. "By the way, my name is Jake." He extended his hand.

"Hi, Jake. I'm Angel." I gently shook his hand.

"Nice to meet you, Angel."

"Nice to meet you, Jake." I smiled.

"I could use so many corny lines right now with your beautiful name."

"Like what?" I batted my eyelashes like a schoolgirl.

"Can I borrow your cellphone?"

"Why?" I shrugged.

"I need to phone Heaven and tell God I found his missing angel."

I giggled. "Yeah, you're right, corny."

"Can I take your picture?"

I scrunched my forehead in confusion.

"I want to prove to my friends that angels really do exist."

My face flushed. I looked at my feet, away from his hypnotic gaze.

"I have lots more—"

"No, that's okay," I interrupted.

"Someone doesn't like my corny one-liners?" He chuckled.

I just smiled.

"They'll grow on you eventually," he replied with a twinkle in his eyes.

"You sound so certain of yourself."

"I am," he replied with confidence. "I am."

***

The first year of our relationship was amazing. Jake spoiled me with attention, gifts, vacations—everything. He treated me like a queen. I wanted to spend every waking hour with him, and I missed him the moment we were apart.

I should've recognized the warning signs back then, but I was so blinded by love I overlooked them. I wish I had known then what I know now. It would've saved me years of my life, my sanity, my self-confidence, a lot of tears, and heartache.

I'll never trust a man again. He has taken that from me. I'll never be the same.

Words

I remember that night like it was yesterday. The memories were raw. I'd never been so scared for my life. He'd had too much to drink that night, like most nights.

But that night was much different than the others. That night, I feared for my life. That night, I thought it was over. That night, he came after me with a hammer.

***

Jake was easy-going, confident, and funny. He could light up any room with his charm and stories. He was a fantastic storyteller—detailed and quite animated. He could grab anyone's attention, especially kids, with his crazy imagination and all his different imitations. Kids absolutely adored him. They loved his stories. Their eyes remained glued and mesmerized as he told funny stories of the fly that forgot his name, the musical monkey, houses being haunted, and fighting off zombies.

But I later learned why he was such a good storyteller. *He was an amazing liar.* And he believed his lies. I even started to believe them. It's hard to explain. Some people are horrible liars; you can tell right away. But others are master manipulators. And Jake was the best of the best.

I don't know how I was so naïve. I don't know how I didn't see the signs and how he twisted *everything*.

It's weird how I started to believe I was the crazy one, how it was my fault, how I was to blame.

He was diabolical. He was evil.

But he wasn't always like that. He had been kind, sweet, and caring. I thought I'd hit the jackpot with him. I thought it was too good to be true. But you know what they always say. *If it's too good to be true, it probably is!*

That night will forever be etched into my brain, like a tattoo. But not a tattoo to admire, this is a tattoo of regret, pain, and absolute fear. I wanted to break the chains of captivity and peel back the layers of negativity that had built up over time. The walls I had once constructed had come crumbling down after meeting Jake. Now I was just a scared child on the other side of an imaginary defenseless wall with no protection from the blows of hurtful words and fists of black-and-blue fury.

I always remembered how the saying goes. *Sticks and stones will break your bones, but words will never hurt you.* That's bullshit! Words sting! Bruises eventually fade away, but, of course, the fear never does. Hurtful words bury themselves deep into the subconscious, like a stubborn splinter.

Words, you never forget. Words will haunt your thoughts and dreams. Words will destroy you.

All I wanted was to be free. I wanted to smile again, to be happy, to laugh. I wanted to feel alive and bubbly, not miserably dead inside. I felt like a prisoner in my own fucked-up head. I desperately tried to keep myself together, but I could feel the stitches holding me together slowly ripping apart at the seams.

Jake had squeezed every drop of life from me. All my hopes and dreams had vanished into a thick fog of despair. My depression worsened by the day, and I no longer knew how to crawl from the dark hole I had dug myself into. I cried myself to sleep most nights, sobbing uncontrollably and desperate to know how I had let myself get here, how I had let a man control me, to bring me down, to crush my soul.

I sit on the sofa, a drink in hand, drowning myself with the poison I despised—the irony. The very thing that turned the man I loved into a monster is now my escape, my go-to when I'm lonely or feeling bad about myself.

It's a way to forget, a way to cope, a love/hate relationship. It's toxic. It's poison. But I can't say no.

FAT PIG

"Who will want to be with you? Look at you. You're fat," Jake said with disgust.

"I'm not fat," I replied softly, lowering my head.

"You're not skinny. You do a good job hiding it with your bulky clothes."

"It's not as easy losing weight after you have a baby."

"I see plenty of women bounce right back to pre-baby weight."

"I've tried, Jake. I've tried several diets. I regularly go on long walks. I've lost twenty pounds."

"But you gained fifty pounds, Ang."

My eyes flooded with tears, and I tried to blink them away. I couldn't let him see me cry. I quickly wiped the tear and donned a weak smile. "I'll do better, I promise."

"How? How will you do better?"

I paused, searching for the right answer. "I'll work out every day, if I have to. I'll eat healthier, maybe even skip meals."

"You need to stop eating so many damn sweets. You know sugar turns to fat, don't you? You need to eat salad. No more burgers or tacos. You look disgusting."

"I'm sorry."

"You should be. I used to be attracted to you. I couldn't keep my hands off you. Now I vomit in my mouth when you take off your clothes."

A hard lump formed in the back of my throat. I pinched myself, trying to dam the tears.

"Are you going to cry?" Jake asked through clenched teeth.

"No." I looked away.

"It's called tough love. Everyone else will lie to your face, tell you how great you look. Do you want me to lie to you, or do you want me to be honest?"

I needed to regain my composure before I spoke. He'd get angry if I started crying.

"Answer me, dammit!"

"I want you to stop being so mean. I'm trying, Jake, I really am. I've lost twenty pounds in three months."

"It's not good enough. Have you seen yourself in the mirror lately?"

"Yes." I sniffled.

"Do you think you look sexy?"

"No."

"How do you expect me to get turned on if you look like this?"

"I'll do better. I promise."

"You know what? I went in to pay for my gas the other day, and the girl behind the counter flirted with me. She was hot. Why can't you be skinny like her? Why don't you flirt with me like that?"

"I've never been a flirt. It makes me feel uncomfortable. You know that."

"Well, I like it. Maybe next time she flirts with me, I'll bend her over the counter and fuck her hard and make you watch."

I couldn't stop the tears anymore.

"I'm just being honest. Would you rather me lie to you? Tell you how hot you look and how much you turn me on? I try to spare your feelings sometimes, but I don't think you're trying hard enough."

I sobbed uncontrollably.

"You better stop, or I'll smack the tears right out of you."

I tried to choke back my tears. I used my sleeve to wipe my nose.

"You want to know why we haven't had sex in three months? Because I don't find you attractive anymore. You know that fat people disgust me. I can't even fake it. The last time we had sex, I had to think of someone else just to get hard."

I couldn't take his hurtful words any longer and ran from the room, crying.

"Don't you dare walk away from me when I'm taking to you! You're weak. You can't handle the truth. You'd rather me to lie to your face."

I heard his footsteps storming up behind me.

He clenched my shoulder and spun me to face him. His fist hit me hard, and everything turned black.

FEAR OF WATER

The fear builds as I frantically try to keep my head above the water as it bobs up and down; my arms thrash like a fish out of water.

I can't swim.

The ground is endless, miles from reach. I panic, gasping for air. My arms and legs are tired. I need to rest; my body's weak, and I can't keep paddling for much longer. The ice-cold water burns my skin, and a sharp pain pierces my legs as the cramps become unbearable.

I scream, but there is no sound. Water rushes down the back of my throat and nose as I choke through my tears. The fear builds to new extremes when I realize I'm going to drown.

A dreadful way to die.

My body tingles like pins and needles—a coldness, raw and deep. I feel my blood turning to slush. My breathing becomes shallow and my head full of fuzz as I'm swallowed into a dark dungeon of emptiness.

***

I awake abruptly, drenched in sweat. The oscillating fan I run at night for white noise sends shivers through me as it sweeps by. I glance at the alarm clock on my dresser—3:24 a.m. Of course, I'm wide awake now.

The recurring nightmare has haunted my dreams for many years. Sometimes it's me drowning, and other times it's someone else, but I can never tell who. I just witness it and feel utterly hopeless, because I can't do anything to stop it. But, worst of all, sometimes I'm the one drowning someone. A deep chill resonates through me. I can't shake the dreadful feeling. The fear of drowning is always so frighteningly real when I'm asleep but fades quickly when I'm awake.

I hate water. I hate boats. I even hate baths.

I began taking showers at a very young age. Bath time was a real struggle for me growing up. I never liked being submerged in water, not even a little bit. The anxiety and fear were overwhelming. I could turn a nice, clean, dry bathroom into a tidal wave of disaster within seconds. You'd think someone was trying to drown me. I'd scream bloody murder at the top of my lungs.

The police came a few times. Concerned neighbors thought my parents were beating us. The police questioned them, and my parents denied any wrongdoing. My mother tried explaining, but it just never came out right. She was embarrassed and didn't know how to control me, even as a young toddler.

I've wondered every day what it would be like if they were still here. My heart had a gapping empty hole I've tried to fill ever since. And possibly the reason I fell so hard for Jake, even though he was terribly wrong for me. I desperately craved affection. All I wanted was to be loved. And he took advantage of that.

But death does something to you; it tears you apart into tiny, little pieces, and you spend the rest of your life trying to put yourself back together. The glue lasts for a little while, but then you just fall apart, sometimes a little at a time, other times you turn into an avalanche and destroy everything in your path. Either it comes as a light mist or a downpour. There's no in-between.

Somedays I was happy, and things were going great, other days I sobbed uncontrollably. It was a battle, but I was a strong person, and I could handle any turbulence that got thrown at me. Whether it be big or small, I was ready for it.

Or so I had thought.

BREAKFAST DISASTER

I turned to look at Jake, fast asleep without a care in the world. How many nights I laid in bed, pissed off at him for how easy he could fall asleep. I was the complete opposite. I lay awake for at least an hour before my mind lets me drift off to dreamland, sometimes longer.

He'd wake up with a good night sleep, and I'd be so miserably tired I just wanted to cry. But I got up, made his coffee and started on breakfast, like a good little wife. I had to make breakfast every morning before he left for work. He slapped me once for setting a bowl of cereal on the table in front of him, but I was just too tired to put any effort into cooking a big breakfast. I hardly slept, and my body desperately needed more. Shocked at his reaction, I stepped backward and touched my cheek—my eyes wide.

"Oh, please. That didn't hurt. I barely touched you," Jake said. He reached for my hand, and I pulled away. He stood from his chair, grabbed the bowl of cereal and dumped it over my head, laughing. He walked around me and into the kitchen. He reentered room and threw the dish towel at me. "Now clean yourself up and make me a goddamn breakfast."

I did as I was told. I wiped my face with the dish towel then soaked up the milk that had spilled onto the floor and quickly blotted the tear before Jake saw me crying. I washed up in the shower and came downstairs to see Jake sitting on the couch, watching a porn and jerking off.

He turned his head to look at me. "Sit down."

My gaze shifted from him to the TV and back to Jake. "*Sit down!*"

I flinched and sat.

"Now watch. Watch what she does to him. If you did that to me, I wouldn't have to watch this and get myself off. You're my wife. Your duty is to please me."

I looked at the floor.

"Watch!" He firmly grabbed my chin and turned my face toward the TV. "Why don't you talk to me like that? It turns me on. Look how hard I am." He grabbed my hand and put it on his hard dick. "You never make me hard like this. Because you're a fat, disgusting pig who doesn't know how to have fun." He slapped me. "You're ruining the mood. Go make my breakfast."

I stood, wiping the tear when I left the room. I sat on the kitchen floor, my knees to my chest, and rocked back and forth, staring at nothing while tears streamed down my face.

THE HAMMER

A stupid argument led to one of the most terrifying nights of my life. I should've known better than to argue with Jake when he'd been drinking. But he was always drinking—always had an excuse. But did that give him the right to do whatever he pleased, knowing I would bite my tongue, wouldn't talk back or argue? I was tired of biting my tongue and silently seething. But he always was a master at turning everything around, like it was my fault. Like I was to blame.

He was perfect. I was a disaster.
He was right. I was wrong.
He was smart. I was stupid.

***

It was late and Jake had been drinking. He was playing music through my iPod speakers, but something went wrong. The speakers would malfunction from time to time. All he had to do was shut it down, leave it turned off for five seconds, turn it back on and poof, the problem was fixed. But tonight, Jake was overly frustrated by the songs not playing smoothly. He eventually got so angry, he threw my iPod on the ground and smashed it, cracking the screen.

I got upset and asked him to apologize.

He kept implying it wasn't his fault. If the damn speakers would work, he wouldn't have thrown it and broke it.

Nothing was ever his fault.

I kept pleading with him to apologize for what he'd done, telling him I didn't care my iPod was broken; all I wanted was an apology. It was my iPod, not his, and he broke it; it's the least he could do. But apparently, he had nothing to apologize for, because it wasn't his fault. He had gotten mad, like he often did after a night of drinking too much.

He entered the spare bedroom off the living room and grabbed something.

I glanced around the corner to see what he was doing and noticed his tool bag sitting on the floor.

He grabbed a hammer from it and came after me.

I gasped, my eyes wide with fear. I backpedaled, afraid of what he would do if I turned and ran from him.

His eyes were wild and full of rage.

My heart hammered as tears welled in my eyes. I held my breath, terrified. I tripped over something on the floor, lost my balance and fell against the window, breaking it.

Jake startled and snapped from whatever trance he was in for just a split second, giving me the chance to flee.

I ran up the stairs, almost tripping and falling on my face. I regained my balance, ran into our bedroom and locked the door. I leaned against the door, sliding down it. I sat on the floor, hugging my legs, and buried my face into them as I bawled; tears streaked my cheeks, now wet with hurt and fear. I heard the thunderous sound come rushing up the stairs, sending bursts of echoes throughout the house.

Jake tried to turn the doorknob and realized it was locked.

I held my breath, paralyzed with fear. The room fell silent, like he was thinking of what to do next. Then, without warning, my body was slammed forward, and I heard a loud crack. I stumbled and fell on my hands and knees. I scanned the room for something but was unsure of what. Another load crack erupted and ricocheted off the walls, sending one of the pictures crashing to the floor. I gasped, covering my mouth.

"You better open this door now, before I come in there and beat your face in."

"Go away!"

"If you don't open this door right now, I'll beat it down, and you'll have what's coming to you."

"Leave me alone. You're drunk!"

Jake laughed an evil, sinister laugh that sent chills to the bone.

I shuddered. He had totally lost it, and I squeezed my eyes shut, wishing it all away.

Will he beat in my face with the hammer or crack my skull wide open?

Will I bleed out on this floor?

Will I whisper my last breath tonight?

"Open the door, Ang!"

Another crack—this time his foot came through the door. He withdrew his foot and ripped out the broken wood with his hands. He reached in and unlocked the door.

His eyes were wild, exploding with red. He grabbed the back of my head and dragged me from the room by my hair.

My scalp felt like it was on fire. I screamed in pain.

He released my hair, and my head slammed against the floor with a painful thud. "Shut up, you dumb bitch!" He drew back his fist then smashed it into my face.

Everything turned black.

Nightmare

Life isn't fair. One second, you're happy, floating on cloud nine; the next instant, the rug is pulled right from under you, falling face first into the ground with a mouthful of dirt and spitting out rocks and sometimes teeth. Worst of all, sometimes it doesn't stop there; it keeps happening over and over again, enough times you don't feel like you can't stand again. How can one person endure so much and yet that stranger standing in front of you in line has never had to deal with one single heart-wrenching, soul-breaking earthquake?

It's just not fair. Life is not fair. Sometimes I wish I'd never been born. A terrible feeling, but my heart hurts so terribly bad sometimes I feel like ripping it from my chest and taking a hammer to it, one blow after another, or taking a shard of glass and cutting it so deep it can't bleed anymore. Maybe then it would stop beating, and I could die in peace, because I know for damn sure I'm not allowed to live in peace. It's just not in the cards for me.

***

I peel open my eyes and survey the room. The walls are bare, and the room is tiny. I sit upright, my back sore from the small sliver of mattress that lays on the metal slab. I shuffle to the wall where a stainless-steel mirror hangs. It's not a normal mirror with glass. It's an unbreakable mirror. I know this first hand, because many times I've slammed my fists, trying. But they won't let us have anything in our room that can cause us or anyone else harm. I don't even get a window. How much I crave sunlight, but all I get is suffocating darkness in this hellhole.

I smell something rancid and sour. I then realize that terrible smell is coming from me as I run my hands down my greasy, knotted hair and raise my armpit for a sniff, repulsed by the pungent smell. *When was the last time I showered? And what am I doing here?* I scan the room for answers but get nothing.

I gasp and whip my head in the direction of the god-awful sound. It bounces off the concrete walls and echoes inside my head as I clamp my hands over my ears to muffle the sound. It sends electric chills down my spine. I kick and scream when I realize the sound isn't coming from someone else, it's coming from me.

***

I awake up abruptly from the nightmare drenched in sweat—a recurring nightmare I've had for many years. I'm not sure why I continue to have these horrible nightmares, but they're never the same. Sometimes I'm sitting in a room, talking to someone I can't see, sometimes just a silhouette of a dark shadow, other times I can see their body but not their face; it's just blank and devoid of features, just a blur. Other times I sit in complete darkness and hear the voice. It's the same voice every time—a gentle, soft-spoken female voice. She asks lots of questions. Sometimes I answer, and sometimes I stay silent, just staring blankly. But, once I'm awake and realize it's just a dream, I can never remember the questions or my answers. All I'm left with is gapping empty holes in my memory. I so desperately try to dig deeper and deeper into my self-conscious mind.

The mind and brain like to play tricks on me sometimes. They do an amazing job to hide the very thing I so fiercely want to find, slowly forgetting everything and everybody that ever hurt me. But what if I don't want to forget? What if I want to remember all those precious moments I try so hard to cling onto, things I don't want to ever forget, but, with every passing day, they continue to slip from my mind until eventually I won't remember any of it—the good, happy memories or the bad and terrible ones. I don't get to choose which ones to hold onto; they all slip away until I remember *nothing*.

THE LAKE

I couldn't sleep last night. I tossed and turned, unable to get comfortable no matter what position I lay in. I awoke from a sound sleep at 2:12 a.m. and couldn't fall back to sleep until after 5:00 a.m. Unsure of what was keeping me awake, an overwhelming feeling of dread ran deep into my veins and rippled through me like a wave of despair and sorrow mixed cruelly together on a canvas.

Something was seriously wrong.

If I could only turn back time. If I would've left him when he had become violent and had morphed right before my very eyes, before he had started to drink too much. If only …

***

The day started perfectly—sunny and beautiful. We decided to take a trip north to a secluded lake for a family canoe trip, just Jake, Courtney, and me. We packed a picnic. Jake had been sober for twenty-one days now. This was the longest stretch he had been without a drink, and things had returned to normal. The hurtful words had stopped, and he hadn't hit me in weeks. Things were good. I was nervous, and my anxiety was through the roof, but Jake always insisted I needed to conquer my fear of water, that nothing bad would happen.

We were floating on the calm lake all by ourselves, smiling and laughing. We stopped in the middle and ate the lunch we had packed—ham and cheese sandwiches, baby carrots, and red grapes. Courtney was six months old now.

But after an hour on the lake, Jake acted different. I had suspected he had possibly poured a shot of vodka into his coffee when we had stopped at the convenient store to fill the gas tank. He had gone inside and was in the store for quite some time. He had said he had to use the bathroom, but someone was using it and waited for a while. He had been acting awkward when he got back in the car.

I had taken Courtney inside to change her diaper, and, when we had returned to the car, Jake seemed overly relaxed. He had been on edge the last few weeks from drying out, which was understandable. I had learned the symptoms of withdrawal to expect from Al-anon—a support group for the families and friends of alcoholics. I had decided to go, hoping my attempt would push Jake into going to AA himself. But Jake had refused; he had claimed he didn't have a drinking problem. He could stop whenever he wanted.

During the last twenty-one days of sobriety, Jake had snapped a lot and had no patience. But at least the name calling and physical abuse had stopped. I could handle this new behavior. But, when I had walked from the bathroom to convenient store's exit, the tiny bottles of liquor had caught my attention. I had just smiled at the cashier, pushed through the door and returned to the car.

Now, a couple hours later, Jake was acting different, like he'd had a few drinks.

"Is everything okay?" I took a bite of my ham and cheese sandwich.

"Yeah of course." Jake smiled, but it seemed forced.

I smiled back suspiciously then gazed across the calm water that sparkled from the sunlight, the canopy of trees that hung over the lake, and the blanket of clouds that drifted across the sky in its obscure shapes. I couldn't have ask for a more perfect day.

Courtney was cranky. It was her naptime, and we should be heading home. She could fall asleep on the two-hour drive home, but Jake insisted we stay, since we didn't do this very often.

Courtney was now crying, and Jake became very irritable, begging me to get her to stop.

"We should go," I insisted. "Courtney needs her nap."

"No! I'm not letting that little bitch ruin our trip. We haven't come to the lake in over a year. She can hang on a little while longer." Jake crossed his arms.

"It's okay, sweetie." I bounced her in my arm, but Courtney continued to cry, and Jake got more frustrated. "Let's just go, Jake. We can come back another time."

"I told you no already. We're enjoying ourselves. She won't ruin this for us."

"*Shh*, sweetie, it's okay. Just lay down your head and sleep," I whispered in her ear as I ran my fingers through her little curls.

"You need to stop babying her so much. This is why she acts this way."

"What's wrong with you today? She's a baby, for crying out loud. What do you expect?"

"Nothing, except she won't shut up and let us enjoy ourselves."

"She's just tired, that's all. Once we get in the car, she'll fall right to sleep."

"You better make her stop before I do!"

"*Shh*, it's okay, sweetie," I whispered, rubbing her head. "Keep your voice down, and maybe she'll fall asleep."

"Did you just tell me to keep my voice down? If she wasn't crying, I wouldn't have to raise my voice! We're just trying to have a good time, but she has to ruin our trips every time! You should've just left her with a babysitter."

Whenever Jake raises his voice, it really upsets Courtney and makes her cry even louder.

"It's okay, sweetie. Just close your eyes."

I saw a look in Jake's eyes that terrified me worse than the night he had come after me with a hammer. He grabbed Courtney and launched her into the lake.

My eyes went wide with fear, but I was paralyzed. I hated water, and the time I had almost drowned as a kid flashed before my eyes.

Courtney was struggling to keep her head above water, flailing her arms and choking on the water.

"Get her, Jake! She's going to drown!"

"You can jump in and save your precious daughter yourself?"

"I can't. I don't know how to swim. We'll both drown!"

"Well, I guess she drowns then."

I had to think quick, or Courtney would drown. *All I have to do is reach Courtney, grab her, swim back to the canoe and hang on for dear life, but could I make it? Doggy paddle, I could manage that. But would I get to her in time? Couldn't be that difficult.*

I jumped out. And that's the last thing I remember.

DEAD

I never knew what really happened to my sweet, sweet Courtney. I don't remember anything after I jumped into the water. Jake claims the paddled to us and grabbed ahold of my hand and pulled me into the canoe, but Courtney had started sinking to the bottom of the lake before I reached her, so he jumped in after her. He tried to give her CPR, but it was no use; she was dead. He carried me to the car and laid me in the back seat, grabbed his phone and called 9-1-1. The police and ambulance took over twenty minutes to reach the lake, since we were in a secluded, desolate area.

Had this been Jake's plan all along, to rid Courtney from our lives, so he could have me all to myself? He had never liked her or all the attention I gave her, and he always said I babied her. What did he expect? He always called her a brat and told her to shut up, complaining how much noise she made, and she cried a lot; she was a colicky baby.

I don't understand it. He had absolutely adored her when she was born. I would just sit there and stare at the two of them. He used to give her raspberries on her belly, and she'd just smile and giggle. She had the most adorable little laugh. He would read her books and rock her to sleep.

Sometimes I couldn't get her to stop crying, but the second he picked her up, she would stop almost instantly. She was definitely daddy's little girl. And I loved it. I wasn't jealous one bit. It made my heart melt into a gooey mess of sugary sweetness. I was head over heels in love with them.

I should've left him when things worsened, but I always made excuses for him. It was the alcohol doing this to him. If only he would stop drinking, I could have my old Jake back. I didn't understand why he had to drink so much. Was his life that miserable?

He blamed Courtney for most of his drinking, said he couldn't handle all the crying. But he drank even when she wasn't. He had an excuse for everything. He said it was never his fault, and he didn't have a drinking problem. But that wasn't the case. After a big fight, he would promise to stop drinking. That would last a day or two.

His drinking got so bad I threatened to leave him many times. He begged me not to, said we just needed a break, to get away, go on vacation and leave Courtney with my sister. But we never did.

Our family was shattered the day he drowned Courtney into the lake. I finally left him and tried to start my life over; however, I spent the next ten years institutionalized, because I had tried killing myself after Courtney died. I took a bunch of pills and drank half a bottle of liquor.

I wish I could take it all back, turn back time and never look back.

He destroyed me. He destroyed us. He killed our daughter.

But he had gotten away with murder. It was his word against mine. And since I don't remember anything after I jumped into lake, the police had said my statement was inadmissible in court. I had blacked out and had gone into shock. It was days before I would speak to anyone.

The police had said that what I had claimed to remember before I had blacked out could just be an illusion I had concocted. It was all very fuzzy. They had convinced me that what I had suggested Jake had done were some serious allegations and had no proof to back it up. Jake even had the police fooled.

Jake had no criminal record, and the police had never been called for domestic abuse. The night he had smashed my face and broke my nose, my whole face had swelled and turned black and blue. Jake had refused to let me leave the house until I healed. He had called out of work sick for a week and watched me like a hawk. I should've called the police, but I was afraid of him. He had threatened to kill us. He had even threatened to set the house on fire while me and Courtney were sleeping.

I feel like I have no one to turn to. And Jake had ensured that. He made me believe my friends were using me, that he was a good judge of character, that my friends only called or wanted to hang out because they had ulterior motives. He said I was a terrible judge in character.

But he knew I wanted to leave him, that I was talking to family and friends, and he didn't like that. He wanted me all to himself. He wanted complete control. He didn't want me to have a support system. He wanted to tear me down and break me. He wanted me to believe he was all I had and that I couldn't live without him.

It took killing my daughter for me to finally leave him. And I'm only to blame for that. I had a choice. I should've seen the signs. But I was convinced if he stopped drinking, things would be the way they had been in the beginning. But his addiction was stronger than anything. And I think because he had no control over his life he tried even harder to control me. And the more I pulled away, the tighter he squeezed.

***

A glimpse of movement from the corner of my eye catches my attention. I whip my head around, but nothing is there. An overwhelming feeling of sadness engulfs. I know who it is; Courtney is visiting me again. She seems to appear in times I feel like there's no reason to live anymore, when I'm sad and alone, like she wants to protect me, to let me know she's still here with me. There were times I wanted to take my life, to be with her again, to stop all the pain and suffering. But my mind gets pulled in two different directions. I'm a strong believer that if I took my own life, I'd never see my Courtney again. I'd go somewhere else. I'd be stuck in the in-between, unable to pass over.

Suicides go somewhere else.

Suicides are punished for all time and eternity.

Suicides suffer alone—forever.

THE SCREAMS

My eyes fly open, but I'm surrounded by darkness. An ear-deafening scream rattles inside my skull, spiraling shivers through my core. It's what must have woken me from a sound sleep. The scream was terrifying, something from a horror film.

Maybe someone's being tortured?

I clasp my hands over my ears to muffle the sound, but it doesn't help much. The screams seem to get louder and closer. I hear loud thumping.

What is that?

My eyes adjust to the darkness a little, and I can barely decipher something. I stumble to my feet, my back and neck stiff. I hate this mattress; it's paper thin.

I grab the bars and lean into them, trying to focus. I see a shadow being dragged down the hallway, kicking and screaming. I gasp. I hear whispers between the screams. The place is coming alive. The scream lessens when the shadows disappear, and a loud slam erupts, rattling the bars.

I need to get out of here, to sleep in a normal bed again. I don't even remember the last time I slept through the night. This place messes with my head. Even the sanest person would slowly dwindle away and turn to dust here.

I've dreamt a thousand ways to end my life, but, with every attempt, I fail. I run my fingers along the jagged scar above my wrist, remembering the last time I tried. My psychiatrist accidently dropped her pen at the end of our session. It rolled off and disappeared under the table. I felt around with my foot and clamped it under my toes and slowly slid it in my sock. When I stood to leave, my pant leg covered the evidence. Later that night, when the lights went out, I grabbed the pen from under my mattress where I had hid it, jabbed it into my forearm and ripped my skin from the bone. I cringed; the pain was too much to take, and I yelped in pain. I felt the warm liquid run down my arm. I laid my head on the pillow and let my arm hang off the side. When I closed my eyes, a smile crept across my face. The sound of keys jangling awoke me later. I had lost a lot of blood but not enough to kill me. Another attempted failure on my record. They would never let me out of here.

I collapse onto the bed and release a sigh. It's been a while since my last attempt, maybe six months. I need to be smarter, more creative. I lie in bed, imaging all the crazy ways I could end it all, end this miserable life, trapped in a cage like a vicious animal.

Tonight, I'll try to crack open my skull on the concrete wall again. They relocated me from the padded room a few weeks ago. I promised I wouldn't try harming myself again. I lied, like I do every time. It's only a matter of time before I try it again. And tonight, is the night.

PART II

NEXT DOOR

I peeled my eyes open—sleepy seeds caked in the corners of my eyes—as the morning light streamed through my bedroom window. The sound of car doors slamming and echoes of banging woke me from a sound sleep. My head pounded, and my mouth felt like sandpaper. I grabbed the half-empty water bottle sitting on my nightstand and swallowed every drop.

I swung my legs over the side of the bed and slid my feet into the slippers on the floor in front of me. I stretched my arms over my head and yawned big. I'm exhausted. I mustn't slept very good last night. I remembered waking up a lot.

I shuffled across the floor, too tired to pick up my feet. I reached for my robe hanging on the back of the closet door and threw it on as I traipsed to the window to see what all the racket outside was. I pulled back the gray curtain covered in white and black abstract designs and peered out the window.

A moving truck sat in the driveway across the street, just northwest of my property. A lady who looked not much older than me was unloading boxes. She had dark hair and was much shorter than the guy with her. He was tall and lanky.

I watched them in a daze, my eyes slowly blinking. *Maybe I'll walk over later and introduce myself. It would be nice to get to know a person or two in town.*

I closed the curtain and shambled down the hallway to the kitchen and brewed some strong coffee—*I'm going to need it*. I surveyed the mess I had left out last night—mail scattered across the counter, dirty dishes in the sink, my new grey sweater I had bought the other day draped over the chair, and a half glass of wine. I poured the undrunk wine down the sink. *What a waste*. I shook my head. *What a pigsty!*

Mary would be so disappointed in me, Miss OCD. I bet she never even left a dirty dish in her sink. I couldn't stand looking at the mess and tidied up while my much-needed coffee finished brewing. I swear that thing gets slower every day. It might be time to buy a new one. *What am I thinking?* The coffeemaker is ancient; it was my grandparents. They make much more modern ones now, but I have a thing for antiques. I like to collect them. I have an old antique phone hanging on the wall in the kitchen, an antique radio sitting on an end table in the living room, and a few decorative knickknacks on the shelves. But my most prized possession is an old telephone booth in my study that I transformed into a mini library.

The steam rose from the pot as I poured the coffee into a black ceramic mug. I added two small scoops of sugar and a dash of cream. I sat in a kitchen table chair and thumbed through *Reader's Digest* until I reached the jokes section—my favorite. *A turtle is crossing the road when he's mugged by two snails. When the police show up, they ask him what happened. The shaken turtle replies, "I don't know. It all happened so fast."* I chuckled and sipped my coffee, burning my lips.

Knock, knock.

I looked up from the magazine. *Who could it be?* I took another sip of coffee, set it on the table and sauntered to the back door. I unlocked the deadbolt and pulled it open to a tall, thin man with auburn hair, light green eyes, and a flannel button-down shirt.

"Hi, my name is Eric," he says in a low voice, his prominent Adam's apple moving as he spoke. "We just moved to town. Is your husband home? I could use some help moving our washer and dryer into the basement. They're heavy."

"I'm sorry, but it's just me here."

"That's okay, no worries. Do you know anyone in town who could help?"

"I'm sorry, I don't. I've been meaning to but just haven't gotten around to it. You know how it is."

"Yeah, of course." He smiled. "Nice to meet you … I didn't catch your name."

"Angel."

"Nice to meet you, Angel. I guess we're neighbors now."

"Yeah, I suppose we are." I smiled. "Nice to meet you too, Eric."

"Why don't you stop by this evening, and I'll introduce you to my fiancé Jennifer."

"Sure."

He nodded and walked away.

I entered the kitchen and grabbed my cup of coffee. I gazed out the window, watching the leaves fall from the trees as the wind blissfully carried them away.

This time of year was my favorite—temperatures cooled, the humidity was almost gone, the flies and mosquitoes died off, the cicadas loud buzzing had seemed to stop overnight. The changing colors of the maple and oak trees were my favorite, with vibrant colors of lemon, tangerine, and ruby red.

Tonight, I would pick up an expensive bottle of red wine and bring it to my new neighbors as a housewarming gift. Maybe I'd finally make some new friends in town. I'd been a hermit these last couple years. But I seemed to fit right into this small, little town. Everyone seemed to stay to themselves. No one stopped by when I moved in and introduced themselves, and I didn't go out of my way to introduce myself either.

Weird.

I'd always heard small towns like these were inviting but nosey, wanted to know everything about everyone, but not here. It was much different here. It was eerily quiet, in an almost secretive kind of way. Everyone seemed afraid to come out behind their locked doors. Which now that I think of it seemed quite strange. But who was I to judge?

I shrugged and drank the rest of my coffee. I retreated into the living room and got comfortable on the recliner and picked up the novel I'd been reading while I disappeared into the depths of the pages.

MIRROR OF TRUTH

I gasped, jolting up in bed. I was covered in sweat and panting. *It's just a dream. It's just a dream,* I reminded myself. I lifted my trembling hands, covered my face, took deep, controlled breaths and exhaled slowly.

It's not real, Angel. Get a hold of yourself.

I swung my legs over the bed and felt for my glasses on the nightstand next to me, almost knocking over a half-empty glass of water. My mouth tasted of old pennies. *Gross.* Smacking my parched lips, I chugged the remaining water. But wasn't enough; I needed more. I checked the alarm clock sitting on my dresser—5:51a.m. I kept it across the room, forcing myself to get out of bed to turn it off in the morning, otherwise I'd roll over and fall back to sleep. I'd done that too many times.

I wasn't a morning person at all, just the opposite—a night owl really. I could sleep all day and stay up all night. My internal clock was backward. It was way too early, but I couldn't go back to sleep after that horrible nightmare, the one that haunts me when I think of the day that completely changed my life forever, the day my entire world was turned upside down—the day I lost my baby girl.

I pulled back the window curtain. The sun was just barely peaking from the eastward horizon. The beautiful colors of burnt orange, magenta, and violet painted the sky, and it was breathtaking. I wished I was more of a morning person. I could definitely get used to this.

I rubbed my eyes and yawned. I desperately needed coffee. I ambled into the kitchen and pressed Start on the coffeemaker. I sat at the table, laid down my head and buried my face in my arms. It was entirely too early to be awake right now.

The stillness in the house felt eerie. My mind wandered where I didn't want it to. The cute laughter and echoing pitter-patter of tiny footsteps made my heart ache. The nights I used to dread getting up in middle of the night to hush my crying baby was what I craved most now. What I would give to get it all back.

My tears cascaded down my cheeks like a waterfall, leaving a puddle on the table. I approached the massive mirror hanging in the front entryway and stared back at the reflection that haunts me.

I used to be happy. I used to be beautiful. I used to be a mother.

Now I was just a disastrous mess. I don't even recognize myself. My once-vibrant eyes were now empty, hollowed out, and surrounded by dark circles and deep wrinkles. I'd wasted away, and now what stood before me in the mirror of truth was skin and bone of an old, bitter woman. How could life be so cruel? How could God let these things happen?

But I got my revenge. I got justice for my little girl. I could smile again, knowing he'd never hurt another human being again.

THE STORM

Main Street was deserted, and a light drizzle sprayed from the sky. I pulled my hoodie over my head and stared at the ominous dark clouds that rolled across the sky as thunder rumbled in the distance. The wind blew leaves across the road, and the treetops swayed to its own chaotic rhythm, a warning of the impending storm approaching.

It'd been all over the news the last few days. Everyone had been talking about it—the storm of the century. They were expecting us to lose power for days, possibly weeks. Every town within three hours was sold out of generators. Fuel was dry in most towns, and the ones that weren't, the price had doubled. People had put bulk tanks on their property to hold plenty of fuel.

A week ago, the traffic was ridiculous. Pure chaos. Now the streets were deserted, not a vehicle on the road or a pedestrian. Either everyone had left for the duration of the pending storm or they had hunkered down in their homes with all the necessities—Igloo sleeping bags, plenty of blankets, hats, gloves, firewood, matches, flashlights, batteries, canned food, water, and booze.

Meteorologists predicted up to eighty-three inches of snow in the next three days. To make matters worse, gusts of wind would reach to sixty miles per hour, causing whiteout conditions with zero visibility and ridiculous snowdrifts. The state advised absolutely no travel in the next several days, and the police issued a warning that they would not be assisting anyone who got stuck while traveling in these conditions. After the snowfall, within a few days, temperatures were expected to dip into an artic freeze, the windchill reaching fifty degrees below zero.

The new storm moto was, *Don't Be Stupid. Stay Home.* But we all know there'd be some brilliant idiot who thought they could outsmart everyone and convinced it wouldn't happen to them.

I'd never been so scared in my life. I should've bought a plane ticket out of here, gone somewhere tropical—like Hawaii, the Bahamas, or Belize—or driven halfway across the country, but now it was too late. All airports within five states were closed. Even interstates and state highways were closed now, including Minnesota, North & South Dakota, Iowa, and Nebraska. I was the idiot who decided to stick around, hoping, praying the impending weather was just a scare—a fluke—and we would only get a few inches, that it turned another direction or stopped dead in its tracks.

I checked the radar on my phone's weather app for the hundredth time. It was a big blob of blue with areas of pink. The blue area indicated snow, and each town had numbers announcing the inches of snow expected in that area; the pink areas were expected to get freezing rain. Blue, of course, covered us with the numbers 60-83 inches, and pink surrounded us.

This doesn't look good. My anxiety rose as the tension grew.

My heart hammered in my chest, and my breathing became shallow and quick. My head was now full of fuzz and clouds. I sat on the floor and brought my knees to my chest—rocking, rocking, rocking. I could feel myself spinning out of control. My stomach was doing summersaults. My skin was crawling. My body was trembling.

I needed to relax. I needed to stay calm. I squeezed my eyes shut and took a long, deep breath and held it ...

One—two—three—four—

I exhaled, letting it slowly escape my lips and trying to take back control. I rubbed my temples.

Five—six—seven—eight—

I got to my feet and headed for the kitchen, trying to shake the feeling. I poured a glass of wine and took a sip. The taste was divine. The hint of oak, raspberries, blackberries, and chocolate rolled over my lips as I savored the flavor. Almost instantly, my heart and breathing slowed, and the clouds faded. I walked to my bedroom and slipped on some sweatpants, a hoodie, and warm socks.

I went into the family room, threw a few pieces of wood into the fireplace and struck a match. I grabbed the book I'd been reading—*Vacant Eyes* by Christine Mager Wevik, a local South Dakota author—from off the shelf and curled onto the couch and got lost into the pages.

LIGHTS OUT

I awoke abruptly from a sound sleep. Confused and half asleep, I rubbed my eyes, realizing I had fallen asleep reading on the couch. My neck was stiff, probably from sleeping in a weird position. I'd been falling asleep on the couch a lot lately. I'd probably get a good night sleep if I slept in my bed once in a while. *That's what beds are for.* I shook my head.

The book I'd been reading had fallen to the floor with no bookmark marking my place. *Dammit!* I thumbed through the pages, trying to find where I had stopped. Skimming through the pages, I realized I didn't remember much of anything last night. My head was pounding. I rubbed my temples in a circular motion, trying to relieve the building pressure. Then I saw the empty bottle of wine I had opened last night. I hugged my legs, resting my forehead on my knees. *I hate hangovers.* Had I eaten anything last night? Recalling the evening, I realized I hadn't eaten anything all day, just drank coffee and wine. *Just lovely.* No wonder I felt like I got hit by a train.

I stumbled to my feet and headed into the kitchen in search of anything to make my stomach stop rumbling and aching so bad. I smacked my dry, parched lips. I was in desperate need of water more than food. I opened the fridge and stared at the contents: a jug of spring water, a half-empty milk container, orange juice, and a bunch of Tupperware full of meals I had prepared in case we lost power and couldn't use the oven. The generator would only power the necessities: the fridge, furnace, water heater, and microwave.

I grabbed an apple and poured a glass of orange juice, emptying its contents in seconds and poured another one. Then I remembered the loud crash that had woken me. I glanced out the window overlooking my back yard and noticed a tree had cracked and landed on the shed roof just fifty feet from the house. *Jesus!* At least it hadn't caved in the roof. I'd have to access the damage later. I didn't feel like doing it now. I felt like shit, and all I wanted to do was sleep.

I switched on the TV and flipped to the local news. All I cared about was the weather updates. A map of the United States was splayed across the screen. The Midwest was still in the danger zone.

"Heavy mixed precipitation is expected," the meteorologist said while pointing at our location on the map. "Total snow accumulation is fifty-four to seventy-two inches, and ice accumulation is expected up to two inches, with winds gusting as high as sixty-five miles per hour. Power outages and tree damage are likely. Travel will be nearly impossible, with blowing snow and snow drifts, causing whiteout conditions. Temperatures will drop to fifty degrees below zero overnight. Don't be stupid, stay home."

I sighed and switched off the TV. At least we were only expecting four to six feet of snow now. Much better than the original six to seven feet, I supposed, but still terrible. I frowned as I clenched my stomach rumbling loudly at me.

I returned to the kitchen, grabbed an apple and took a big bite. The crisp, sweet flavor burst in my mouth. I took another big bite, realizing how ravenous I was after being on an empty stomach for nearly a day and a half. I didn't think an apple would suffice.

I made a peanut butter and jelly sandwich, using my grandmother's homemade strawberry jelly. Her pantry was packed of all kinds of homemade jellies, sauces, and different pickled vegetables; she loved to can. I had taken a bunch with me when I had moved out and stored them in my cellar. Every time I opened a new jar, it reminded me of her. I wish she'd passed on her recipes to one of us, but they all died along with her. I tried to use them sparingly. Once they were gone, they were gone forever— no replacing them.

I'd tried making them myself, but it wasn't the same. I failed every time. She must've had a special ingredient or just that special touch I was missing. Some people just had a gift, mine was not cooking. I was a decent cook, especially my homemade alfredo, but I didn't even compare close to my grandmother's cooking. Near the end, she had lost her touch at the onset of dementia. I missed her and my grandfather dearly.

***

The lights had been flickering on and off for the last hour before they finally went out. I pulled the curtain aside and gazed outside. I couldn't see a thing in the dark, just the shadows of trees swaying neurotically in the treacherous wind. I shuddered. The wind blustered fiercely and with full of rage. *Just great!* I should've dragged the generator inside before the storm. Now I must try to reach the storage shed without blowing away.

I grabbed a flashlight, my heavy winter coat, hat, and gloves for my treacherous trek outside. Finally dressed for the Artic, I opened the front door just as the wind caught it and flung it against the house with a loud bang. I struggled with the door before finally getting it closed behind me.

I shone the flashlight, analyzing my surrounding and realizing this wouldn't be easy. The snow drifts would make it difficult to get the generator to the house. I clenched my hat and cursed at myself as I fought against the wind and tromped through big snow drifts, trying to kick a path. The snow pelted my face, stung with its bitter coldness. I reached the shed and dug into my pocket, realizing I had forgotten the key. I cursed at myself and traipsed back to the house, fighting against the wind.

I finally managed to drag the generator outside and struggled through the snowdrifts and wind, almost getting it stuck several times. But I was finally inside, my skin tender and burned red hot. My skin prickled as it revived itself.

It took me several tries before I could start the generator in the cold. My weak arms were no match for the cold jump start. I was a frozen icicle and out of breath, but the furnace was finally running again. My fridge, microwave, and a lamp were plugged in, and the room was lit. I could finally relax.

I grabbed a big blanket from the closet, poured myself some hot chocolate and cuddled on the couch with a book. The moaning and popping of the house startled me. At times, it sounded like someone was beating on the house with a sledgehammer. Then I heard it again, but, this time, I realized it wasn't the house popping, but someone banging on my front door. *Who the hell?*

I slowly opened the door, ensuring to hold tight, so it wouldn't blow against the side of the house again. "Jen!"

"I'm sorry for bothering you, but I saw your lights on. The whole town has lost power, and the temperature in the house has dropped uncomfortably. Can I ride the storm out here with you?" Jen shivered, rubbing her arms.

"Of course!"

"Thank you. You're a lifesaver." Jen unzipped her jacket, pulled off her gloves and put them inside her hat. She shoved them into the coat arms before hanging it up.

"Would you like a glass of wine?"

"I would love one. Thanks." Jen smiled.

I topped off two glasses of wine and handed one to Jen.

"What's going on, Angel? You seem distracted and down today." Jen tilted her head and eyed me quizzically then sipped her wine.

"It's nothing." I forced a smile and looked at my hands as I picked at my fingernails.

"I know you better than that." Jen paused. "I can tell something's on your mind. Sometimes just talking about it can make you feel better."

"You know how the old saying goes? Sticks and stones will break your bones, but words will never hurt you?"

"Well, yeah. Doesn't everyone?"

I sighed deeply and sank into the couch cushions. "I think that's horseshit. Words can haunt you forever." I glanced up and back down again.

Jen frowned but didn't say anything.

"Jake really screwed with my head." I hesitated, shifting nervously in my seat. "He loved to put me down and shred my confidence piece by piece. Any confidence I had left hanging by threads he had severed with a butter knife." I paused. "It wasn't easy at first, but years of emotional abuse will do that."

Jen nodded, taking a sip of her wine, and leaned in.

"He made me feel like I didn't deserve him, that he was better than me, that he was the best I could ever have. He put himself on a pedestal and kicked me down further and further into a hole I couldn't dig myself out of. In the end, I would beg him for just the smallest bit of affection or attention. He made me feel like I should be happy he paid any attention to me at all. That I didn't deserve it. That I didn't deserve him. It was sick and twisted."

"He was an asshole, Angel. You shouldn't let him bring you down. You're better than that." Jen forced a smile.

"In the beginning of our relationship, I had confided in him my insecurities, that he later used against me to break me down. He manipulated me into believing he cared about me." I leaned over, picked up my wine, hand trembling, and took a sip. "He used to tell me how beautiful I was and how lucky he was to have me in his life. When we first started dating, he cooked me five-course meals, took me on two-hour canoe trips up north on a quiet lake all by ourselves, bike rides in the country, and long walks. He had asked me what I wanted in life and what made me truly happy. He had been eager to know everything about me and listened intently. He had told me I could achieve anything I put my mind to, that he believed in me, that he loved me for who I was, and he wouldn't change a thing about me. He'd play love songs and dance with me all night long as he whispered sweet nothings into my ear."

I quickly swiped away a tear. "But nice Jake had lasted only the first two years of our relationship, long enough for me to believe he truly loved me and wanted to spend the rest of his life with me. But the text messages he used to send me throughout the day, telling me how much he missed me and couldn't wait to see me, stopped. The little love notes he had left around the house eventually stopped. He always would wake me and kiss me before he left for work every morning and tell me he loved me."

I sighed deeply and sniffled. "He morphed into a selfish, controlling, and abusive man—physically, emotionally, and sexually. He coerced me do things to him that made me feel *very* uncomfortable. He told me if I loved him I would do it. Otherwise, he would find someone else to take care of his sexual desires and would make me watch."

Ashamed, I lowered my head. "He was addicted to gambling, porn, and alcohol. Once, he blew through twenty grand in one night at the casino."

Jen gasped, bringing her hands to her mouth.

"He would tell me all the time how boring I was and how I didn't know how to have fun. How he was the life of the party. And he was God's gift to women, and he could have any woman he wanted. And he didn't know why he had settled down with a fat pig who didn't know the first thing about having fun. He even threatened to bring home another woman and fuck her in our bed on several different occasions. The man I trusted with everything had turned into a monster." I sobbed into my hands, ashamed to look at Jen.

Jen wrapped her arms around me and let me cry it out.

After I calmed down, I pulled away and wiped my face with my sleeve.

"Angel, Jake was cruel, and he knew how to get under your skin. He knew all your insecurities and played them against you. I'm so sorry you had to go through that. No one should have to endure what you did." Jen frowned. "But you're right. Jake was a monster, and you can't keep letting him win."

"How am I letting him win?" I asked, choking on my words.

"After all these years, letting these horrible memories corrupt your thoughts, they are toxic and only will continue to tear you down and destroy you until you let them go and move on."

"I would love to. I hate having these terrible feelings. I want to forget it all. I want to forget Jake. I want to forget Courtney. Their memories only cause heartache. I want to just disappear." I covered my face and sobbed into my hands.

"Oh, Angel." Jen squeezed me tight. "Everything will be okay. Let's forget about Jake and find a healthy distraction."

The lights flickered a few times and then finally stayed on. I downed the rest of the wine in my glass, wiped my mouth and stood. "Let's go bake some cookies." I smiled at Jen, and we walk into the kitchen.

Dinner

It felt like yesterday when Jen moved to town. Honestly, I didn't know what I would've done without her. She had been a true friend; someone I could trust. She had been there for me through the good times and the bad. She understood me. I was definitely not the easiest person to deal with; I had some serious baggage. She could've walked away and not dealt with my crazy ass, but she didn't. She stuck by my side through it all.

I remembered walking to her house the day they had moved here. I had drank a couple glasses of wine before I headed there—okay, maybe three or four. I was shy and needed to take the edge off. I had made chicken alfredo for them for dinner. I knew they didn't have time to cook, since they were unpacking. I thought it would be the nice thing to do.

I realized after I got to their house, I had forgotten the garlic bread in the oven. I ran back inside and to the kitchen, the smoke alarms blaring, and shut off the oven.

The smoke barreled out. I opened a few windows to air out the place.

The thought of my grandmother popped in my head and how she had been in the end, how she had almost burned down our kitchen when we were kids.

I crossed the back yard to their house for the second time tonight and, halfway there, realized I had forgotten the bottle of wine I had bought for them. I shook my head. I was turning into my grandmother.

After the third attempt, I finally arrived at their house, but the alfredo was cold now. I knocked on the door.

A lady much shorter than me—probably 5'2", with brown hair, blue eyes, and a round face—opened the door and smiled. "Hi. You must be Angel."

"Yes. I brought dinner." I handed her the dish.

"That's very kind of you to think of us."

"I figured, with all your things packed up, you'd have a hard time cooking."

"Come in and join us." Jen stepped aside to let me in.

"I have a confession. The food is probably cold by now," I said, embarrassed, looking at the floor. "I had to run home twice after forgetting the garlic bread in the oven, which is burnt to a crisp, and then the wine. I'm sorry." I shook my head as I reached in my pocket for the corkscrew I had managed to remember.

I poured the luscious red wine into our glasses, handed Eric and Jennifer their glasses then picked up mine.

"Wait!" I hollered.

They both froze, expressions of alarm across their faces.

"I want to make a toast." I rose my glass with a smile. "To new friendship, all the embarrassing and awkward moments, and horrible first impressions."

Jen chuckled, and Eric smirked, raising their glasses with a clank. We all took a sip simultaneously. The semi-dry red wine caressed my taste buds with notes of dark cherry, blackberry, and mocha.

"Wow! This is amazing wine, Angel. Where did you get it?" Jen asked.

"At a local winery just outside Toronto called Sylvania."

"It's delicious!"

"I know. It's my new favorite winery. They age their wine in oak barrels for seven years before they bottle them. It adds a distinctly unique flavor to the wine that's remarkable."

"I'd say." Jen nodded and took another generous sip.

"What does a bottle like this cost?" Eric asked, glancing at me.

"Depends, but roughly around eighty dollars."

"Eighty dollars?" Jen coughed, almost choking on the wine she had just swallowed.

"Now, come on, Jen. That's alcohol abuse," I said, trying to tease her, but I don't think it came out the way I had wanted it to.

Her eyes widened, and she covered her mouth. "I'm sorry."

I didn't think she understood my sarcasm. "I'm just kidding."

"Oh," Jen says shyly, looking her feet then at me.

"What I meant was, I'm just kidding with how much the wine cost. It only cost half of that. You think I'd spend eighty dollars on a bottle of wine for people I just met?"

Jen nervously shifted her weight.

"Of course I would." I chuckled. "I would spend triple that for a great tasting wine. You won't find a cheap bottle that tastes anything remotely as good as the more expensive ones." I paused to take another sip. "My favorite types of wine have buttery characteristics, are full-bodied and rich in flavor with a smooth finish."

"Sounds delicious," Jen replied.

I noticed Jen's posture was more relaxed now. I thought she'd assumed I was serious. Poor Jen. She was definitely in for a rude awakening. I was a very complex and stubborn person. But, most importantly, I spoke my mind. And, for some, that could be a hard pill to swallow. The only person I'd ever bit my tongue around was Jake, but he was a raging alcoholic.

The truth hurt sometimes, which I was very aware of. People were so used to hearing what they wanted to hear. But it was a great quality—being brutally honest. Just most people couldn't handle the truth. They'd rather believe a lie. Me. I wanted to know how someone truly felt, not what they thought I want to hear.

I wanted to know peoples inner-most thoughts, the thoughts they were afraid to confess, the thoughts people wished they had the guts to say—raw and unfiltered.

I hated fake people. Jen, thank God, was not one of those people. She was my savior, my saving grace. Sometimes she didn't seem real, the way she showed up when I was at my lowest. I just hoped she wasn't another person too good to be true.

THE PLANNER

I found a daily planner in the back of my desk drawer, a drawer I hadn't opened in years. But just like something had drawn me to that abandoned farmhouse in the forest behind our childhood home, the same feeling drew me to this. I opened the small planner and thumbed through the entries. I saw handwritten on April 22: *Dr. Melville 11:30 a.m.* Who is Dr. Melville? The same name was written on many dates. At first, a couple times a week, then once a week, dwindling to every other week, then it just stopped—a bunch of blank entries.

Curious, I retrieved a phonebook and scanned the yellow pages under Physicians. I came across Dr. Melville Psychiatric Services in Brookings, and my eyebrows furrowed with confusion. I dialed the number and sat patiently as it rang on the other end, then finally, someone answered.

"Dr. Melville's office. How can I help you?" a female voice asked.

I panicked, not knowing what to say.

"Hello?"

I still couldn't find the words trapped in my throat.

"Hello?" the voice said agitated.

"Hi," I blurted before she hung up.

"Can I help you?"

"My name is Angelina Walker. I'm not sure if you can help me." I paused. "I just found Dr. Melville's name in my planner for several appointments two years ago, and I was wondering if I could make an appointment to talk to him."

"Dr. Melville is a woman," the voice said annoyed.

"I apologize. I-I just wanted to know if she could see me sometime soon."

"Dr. Melville just had someone cancel this afternoon. Would three o'clock work for you?"

I paused, panicking, my hands trembling. I wasn't sure if I was ready for this. I didn't realize it would be so soon. "Yes, that works just fine." My voice cracked.

"Okay. I'll put you down for three."

"Thank you," I said softly and hung up.

I stared blankly, my legs bouncing nervously. *How could I forget someone I had so many appointments with?* I took a deep breath and squeezed my eyes shut tight. I couldn't believe I was doing this. I didn't know if I was ready for this—ready for the truth. I exhaled, unaware I had been holding my breath. I stood slowly; my legs felt like Jell-O. I went to the bathroom to get ready, hoping a hot shower would do me some good.

I stood in the shower until the water ran cold and my teeth chattered. I stepped out of the shower, not feeling much better than I had when I entered. I towel dried and got dressed. My stomach was full of knots twisting and trying to suffocate me, maybe warning me I wasn't ready for this. I winced in pain, took a deep breath and held it for several seconds, hoping the pain subsided, but it doesn't.

I must do this, I reminded myself. I couldn't keep hiding from the truth, no matter how much it hurt. All these empty holes in my mind were driving me crazy. I needed to know the truth and why I kept having these terrible nightmares. Maybe the answers would set me free, but, deep down inside, I thought the truth would tear me into pieces.

I climbed into the car, realizing I had left the keys inside, and ran back inside to get them. They weren't where I usually leave them. I search frantically, starting with the kitchen counter, under the couch cushion, upstairs on my nightstand, in the kitchen drawer, but they were nowhere to be found. I looked inside my coat pocket hanging on the hook in the entryway and finally found them there. I ran back outside to try this again. I climbed into the car and backed out of the driveway and headed west.

***

I left Dr. Melville's office feeling nauseated. I didn't get many answers; she said it wasn't her place to tell me everything. She wanted me to read the journal I had her hold onto. She told me after I read it, if I needed someone to talk to, she was just a phone call away. She gave me her personal phone number and said I could call her anytime, day or night. She seemed very hesitant in giving me the journal, which makes me even more nervous than

I already was. Am I really ready to know my innermost thoughts? To know what really had happened? To know why my mind had so many holes and why I have so many nightmares?

The anxiety built on my drive home. I felt like was suffocating, and everything was closing in around me. I kept glancing at the journal sitting so innocently in the passenger seat like it was full of cotton candy and unicorns, but I knew better. It held many secrets, secrets I wasn't so sure I was ready to unleash onto my fragile mind. My hands trembled as I shifted nervously in my seat, trying so hard not to look at the journal. I took a deep breath and squeezed the steering wheel tighter, gazing at the windmills scattered in the distance. The wind turbine blades sliced through the air in a hypnotic rhythm of continuous motion. I rolled down the window and sucked in the fresh air to help me relax.

I slowed and turned onto my street. The downpour we'd had the other night had washed out the town's roads and left behind a terrible mess, my tires slipping and sliding while trying to find traction. I turned into my driveaway and shifted into Park. I released the seatbelt and sighed heavily as I leaned back and stared blankly. The weird sensation built as I tried so hard to avoid looking at the journal. I quickly grabbed it and slid it into my bag. I climbed out of the car and shut the door behind me.

My feet squished in the mud as I approached the front porch and collapsed onto the swing. I heard a low rumble in the distance as the wind whipped my hair. I pulled it back and twisted it into a ponytail to keep it out of my eyes. The chill from the wind sent shivers through me as I stared at the massive decorative-carved white columns on the front porch. My house was beautiful. I couldn't forget how lucky I was, but was I? I didn't feel lucky. I have money, which makes life a little easier, but not luck. I would give it all up in a split second if I had the chance to hold my baby girl again, to look into her big blue eyes and hear her laugh again. I wanted to feel okay again, to stop the pain. I wanted to be happy. I put my hand on the journal and sighed. It held the truth.

I needed to know.

I needed to remember.

I needed to fill all the empty holes.

The sky darkened as thick charcoal-colored clouds rolled in, and a light drizzle fell. I watched the swaying trees and the leaves dancing in the wind. I crossed my arms and rubbed them briskly as bumps formed. I grabbed my bag and walked inside. I dropped my bag on the couch and headed to the kitchen to pour myself a glass of pinot noir. I took a sip of the warm liquid and closed close my eyes and smiled. I returned to living room, set my glass on the coffee table and plopped on the couch, letting my body sink into the cushions.

I grabbed the journal from my bag, set it on my lap and ran my fingers across the cover and down the sides. I thumbed through the pages and stopped, staring at the words.

> *I don't know how much more of this I can take. My brain is full of fuzz and clouds. The nurses keep pumping me with drugs. I'm not well. I have these emotional explosions. I kick and scream*

and slam my head against the wall until everything turns black. I'm going crazy in here, trapped in this hellhole. No windows, no fresh air, or sunlight. One minute I'm screaming and pulling clumps of hair out of my head, the next I'm crying my eyes out and hyperventilating until I vomit, and the next I'm laughing hysterically, laughing so hard my insides hurt. I'm either on the verge of hysteria or a nervous breakdown. But which, I'm not sure. All I know is I deserve much worse. There is no place for me, not even Hell holds a place for someone like me. What I did was unthinkable. What I did was unforgiveable. I deserve to rot in the ground while maggots and cockroaches feed on my flesh until nothing's left of me other than rotted bones.

I slammed the journal shut, panting. I couldn't read anymore. I wasn't ready for this. I wasn't ready for the truth.

What had I done? And where was I when I wrote that? In prison? Why can't I remember? How long was I there? Why don't I remember my therapist or the journal or what I did? I guzzled every drop from my wine glass and went to the kitchen to pour another.

I was torn between wanting to know the truth and wanting to bury the truth forever. But, for now, I would drink until I went numb.

ELLIOTT

A loud rap on the door woke me from a sound sleep. I blinked several times and sat upright. A book tumbled from lap onto the floor. I must have fallen asleep on the couch again. I tried to rub the sleep from my eyes as another loud knock erupted from the door. I stood but leaned over quickly to catch my balance on the couch arm as the room turned to static. I blinked hard as my eyes focused again, and I shuffled to the door in a daze. I unlocked it to see Mary standing there, her head hanging low, and she was sobbing.

My face twisted. "What's wrong?"

"It's Elliott … He's dead!"

"What do you mean?"

"He killed himself."

I gasped.

Mary looked up; her eyes were puffy, and her cheeks were streaked with tears. She removed a folded piece of paper from her pocket and handed it to me with trembling hands.

We walked inside. Mary's unsteady legs wobbled as she stepped.

I put my arm around her waist to help guide her into the living room. We sat on the couch. I grabbed the book from the floor next to my feet and set it on the coffee table in front of me then faced Mary.

She buried her face in her hands and sobbed.

I rubbed her back and felt her body shaking uncontrollably. I still gripped the folded-up paper Mary had handed me. I took a deep breath, trying to prepare myself for what I was about to read. I paused, shut my eyes tight and exhaled. I slowly unfolded the paper one corner at a time, a lump forming in my throat.

> *To, My Beautiful Wife,*
>
> *I am so sorry for what I have done. I cannot live with the guilt a day longer. The guilt has tormented my soul, and I am reminded of how horrible of a man I am every time I look at you and our daughter. I never meant for any of this to happen. I met Ashley at work when she was only twenty-two and an assistant at the firm, and I eventually gave in to temptation and couldn't stop my sexual urges. I was not honest with you about being laid off. I resigned after the firm found out about Ashley, since the relationship was considered against company policy. I was very selfish, and I blame myself for everything that has happened. The guilt is eating me alive. I can't eat or sleep. It is completely consuming me. I trusted Joseph to care for our daugh-*

ter while I slept with another woman against our vows of marriage, and I know this must hurt you immensely. But, worst of all, the man I trusted raped our daughter for three years and got her pregnant. Even though Joseph was found guilty and incarcerated for hurting our little girl, I cannot live with the guilt any longer. I'm reminded of the horrible husband and father I am and how neither of you deserved this. So I am doing what I do best and being selfish by ending the torment that has been eating me alive. I am sorry for everything. You and Natalie will be much better off without me around. You both deserve a better man in your lives. I always loved you, Mary, even if you don't want to believe me.

Goodbye. Elliott.

I gasped. "I'm so sorry, Mary. I had no idea." Tears welled in my eyes, and, when I blinked, they streamed down my cheeks. I wrapped my arms around Mary and squeezed tight, not letting go for several minutes as we both cried.

"I loved him, Angel. I don't care if he had an affair. We could have worked through it … But I blame him for what happened to Natalie." Mary nervously twisted her hands on her lap. "I know he would never do anything to intentionally hurt her, but, because of his choices, she was raped." Mary choked out the words and looked up at me, so much pain behind her eyes.

My bottom lip quivered as I tried to dam my tears. I touched Mary's knee, her leg bouncing. I didn't know what to say. I couldn't say anything to make any of this easier. I just sat and listened as she spilled her heart out to me, admitting the terrible things the kids at school were saying to Natalie and the unbearable rumors that were crushing Natalie's soul. I could feel my heart shatter into a thousand pieces.

We sat and talked for hours, but then Mary noticed the time. She said she must leave. She didn't want Natalie to come home to an empty house.

I escorted Mary to the door and gave her another hug. I waved to her as she backed her car out of my driveway. I closed the door behind me and shambled to the kitchen, poured a strong drink and drowned myself in sorrow until I could no longer see straight.

I laid down and fell deep into the comfort of my bed, sobbing into my pillow until I cried myself to sleep.

THE DARKEST CORNERS

As I brooded over things that should've been left in the past, I clutched my glass, the anger building, wanting to throw it across the room and watch it shatter into a thousand pieces, just as my life had done.

I just couldn't shake the feeling. I could hear him mocking me, an edge to his voice. I sighed heavily as a wave of nausea hit me hard and sent me running into the bathroom. I swallowed hard, trying to fight the urge creeping up my throat.

Heavy emotions filled the empty space around me. The painful memories assaulted my mind. As hard as I tried to push them from my mind, the shadows of the past kept haunting. These memories triggered emotions of deep sadness and utter pain while the poisonous darkness threatened to destroy me. I couldn't keep punishing myself like this. I tried desperately to clutch onto the good memories instead of drowning myself in anguish. Regret seeped into my bones as the guilt rippled through me.

Alcohol had been my best friend throughout the years. It offered me a wonderful distraction and numbed my brain from all the horrible memories that haunted me daily. I must keep reminding myself that I needed to let it go, to move on with my life, but I couldn't. It consumed me. I couldn't keep living like this, or I'd go mad.

I was in a constant battle with the darkest corners of my mind. I'd lost track of the countless times I'd wanted to just put an end to all my pain and suffering. But my fear of never seeing my little girl again was the only thing that kept me going—and the fear that suicides go somewhere else. I didn't blame Elliott for killing himself; I'd wanted to so many times. I couldn't imagine the pain he had been feeling when he finally decided to end it all, to leave my sister and their daughter without a husband and father. Did he too fear he would never see Mary or Natalie again? Or did he not care? Was his guilt and sadness so overwhelming he would rather end the pain than have the chance to ever see them again? This thought scared me, and I tried to push it from my mind.

Suicide was a selfish thing, but the pain and suffering could be so overwhelming, and the dark thoughts that could haunt every day was more than some people could handle. I feared my mind was breaking, and that scared the shit out of me.

I called Jennifer. I should be calling my sister instead, but what good would that do? We were both broken souls.

"Hello?" a deeper voice answered.

"Hi, Eric. It's Angel. Is Jennifer home?"

"She's sleeping. She had to work a double yesterday. She probably won't be up for a while." He paused. "But I can let her know you called when she wakes up."

"Yeah. Okay." I smiled in the receiver, even though he couldn't see it. I hung up and slid my backside down the wall until I reached the floor. I covered my face in my hands and rocked back and forth.

I checked the clock across the room—10:17 a.m. It was entirely too early to start drinking. I needed to do something else to distract my attention before Jen called me back. I stood and paced the room back and forth. *Get yourself together, Angel. Get yourself together.*

After several minutes of pacing, I entered my library, admiring all the novels I own. This put a temporary smile on my face. I scanned the bookshelves, searching for the perfect distraction. After some time passed, one finally caught my attention: *If Tomorrow Comes* by Sidney Sheldon. He was my ultimate favorite author of all time. The title seemed perfect for how I felt at the moment. I have immensely enjoyed each of his novels. I grabbed it off the shelf and sauntered to my reading corner—a window overlooking my massive back yard with a cushioned reading bench and a pillow that contours around my waist. The pillow's faded and cracked black-printed letters read, *Just One More Chapter*. I plopped down and opened the first page.

***

I stopped reading and checked the page number—212. How could that be? I wracked my brain with the pages I had just read but only found cobwebs in the corner of my mind as it kept drifting to someplace else—so much for a healthy distraction. But what thoughts? It was all blank and empty, with big gaping holes of nothingness. I had no idea what I had just read, so I closed the book in frustration and set it on the seat in front of me. I glanced out the west-facing window to see the slashes of orange and pink sprayed across the sky as the sun set. *What time is it?*

I didn't have a clock in my library, because I didn't want the time looming above me, distracting me. If I was reading a book, I wanted to get lost amongst the pages and temporarily escape this treacherous world. How wonderful it felt to escape into the brilliant minds of authors.

I wished I could write a book. But, what would I write about? My terrible life, the terrible things that have happened to my sister and her family, or my parents? I wanted to write a book with unicorns jumping over rainbows and the sun shining ever so brightly in the clear blue sky. Something not about life and how horrible, unfair, and painful it could be. I wanted to write about tooth fairies visiting children while they were sleeping, leaving her fairy dust of happiness on their pillow, so they could breathe it in and believe the world was a good and happy place. But no one wanted to read books like that. I didn't want to read books about that. It wasn't realistic. It was a fake world that didn't exist. But, how desperately I wished I could escape into that world when I felt like ending it all to pretend for just a second I could be happy again.

The phone rang, interrupting my thoughts. I answered after the third ring. "Hello?"

"Hi, Angel, it's Jennifer. Sorry I missed you earlier. Eric said you called." Her voice sounded thick with sleep.

"Yeah, sorry. I didn't realize you worked a double shift."

"A couple nurses called in sick with the flu, so I offered to cover. It's good money with all the overtime, but I was exhausted and falling asleep at the wheel on my way home this morning."

"I bet. How many hours did you end up working?"

"Twenty-four hours." She yawned. "So, what's up?"

"Oh, nothing. I just needed someone to talk to. But I'm okay now."

"Do you want to have dinner with us? I made lasagna."

"I would love that." I smiled. "Sounds delicious. I haven't had lasagna in ages. I'll bring a bottle of wine. What time should I head over?"

"Now, if you wanted. I just put the lasagna in the oven. It should be ready in forty-five minutes."

"Let me jump in the shower and freshen up. I've been lazy today."

"Sure. See you soon."

We hung up the phone, and I smiled.

***

In just twenty minutes flat, I was walking to Jennifer's house, wine in hand. I slowed as I worried I was intruding on their dinner. Maybe this was a bad idea. I didn't need to burden them with my problems. What was I thinking, accepting the invitation for dinner? It wasn't like she had planned on me coming over tonight. She was only being polite, because I had called her earlier, and she had been sleeping. I turned and returned to my house, my head hanging low.

I pulled open the utensil drawer in the kitchen, searching for the corkscrew. After a couple attempts, I finally found it buried in the back. I pressed it into the cork and twisted vigorously then clamped it down as it popped out. I poured the wine to the rim and sat at the breakfast bar, resting my chin in my hand as I stared blankly at nothing. I shook my head, blinked hard and sipped the wine as the taste of dark fruit and notes of chocolate and vanilla rolled over my pallet. I savored the full-bodied, smooth flavor of the delicate wine before I swallowed. *They don't know what they're missing out on.*

My stomach growled angrily. I pondered the last time I had eaten something. I probably should've just gone to Jennifer's; lasagna sounded really good. They *were* waiting for me; it wasn't too late to change my mind. But, the longer I waited, the more hesitant I became. I cracked open a can of salty peanuts from the cabinet and threw them in my mouth. Peanuts compared nothing to lasagna, but it would do. I sat with the can of peanuts and took another handful, feeling famished.

The phone rang. I didn't bother answering it. I know it was just Jen wondering when I'd be there. I took another sip of wine. The ringing continued for what seemed like forever, then it stopped. I sighed heavily and tossed another handful of peanuts into my mouth and chomped away. I stared at my empty wine glass and contemplated pouring another a glass so soon. I couldn't believe I had drunk it that fast. I felt a slight pounding in my head—never good to drink on an empty stomach.

The phone rang again. It rang and rang, and rang some more. I wondered how long it would ring before she finally gave up, then silence filled the room again.

I poured another glass of wine and thought how rude I was. Why would she even want to be friends with me? I was never happy. I griped and moaned about all my problems, but she would patiently listen while I spilled my guts to her. She would just nod and shake her head when I talked, not wanting to interrupt. She was such a great friend, and I was a terrible friend; she had invited me for dinner and then I didn't even show up, and, when she called, looking for me, I didn't answer the phone. I was pathetic. What was wrong with me?

A loud rap on the door interrupted my thoughts, and I startled. I hesitated, but, after the loud rap erupted again, I headed to the door. I unlocked it to see Jen standing there, Tupperware in hand with a smile.

"I tried calling you when you didn't show up for dinner, but you didn't answer."

"I know. I'm sorry." I lowered my head, shamed to look her in the eyes.

"Is everything okay?"

"Yeah, I'm fine."

"Can I come in? I brought some lasagna, if you're hungry."

I stepped aside, so she could enter, still unable to make eye contact.

"Do you want to talk about what's bothering you?"

"Not really. I don't want to be a burden."

"You're not a burden, Angel. You're my friend. That's what friends do. They talk."

Silence fell between us. I didn't know what to say.

"You should eat. You look like you haven't eaten in days."

"I just had some peanuts."

"That's not a meal."

"Peanuts contain a lot of protein."

Jen shook her head and sighed. She retrieved a plate and fork from the cabinet and drawer and set them the counter. She scooped the lasagna onto the plate and nuked it in the microwave. When the microwave beeped, she removed it and set it on the table in front of my wine glass. "Now eat," she demanded with a smile.

I obeyed, not blowing on it first and burning my mouth. I took quick deep breaths in, trying to cool my mouth, but it didn't help much, so I gulped my wine. "It's delicious. Thank you, Jen. You're too kind to me." I shoveled another bite into my mouth, and another, almost swallowing them whole. I was famished.

Jen stood and smiled as she watched me turn into a garbage disposal.

"I'm so rude. Would you like a glass of wine?"

"I would love one."

I grabbed a glass from the cabinet and poured the wine, ensuring not to pour it as generous as mine; she wasn't an alcoholic like me or needed to drown herself in the poison. I forced a smile and slid it across the table as she sat.

"Thank you," she said then took a sip.

We talked for a while, losing track of time. She said she had to leave to get ready for another long shift tonight.

I nodded and walked her to the door, thanking her for the lasagna and apologizing for being such a shitty friend. I closed the door behind her, and, as a tear fell down my cheek, I quickly wiped it away. *I don't deserve her. She's too nice to me.*

I was emotionally exhausted and felt terrible for the way I had treated Jen tonight. I lay in bed, curled up under the blankets, and cried myself to sleep.

THE ZOO

"Mommy, look at the baby cat."

I turned and crouched to her level. I peered through the smudged glass dotted with millions of dirty fingerprints. In the corner under a shaded tree was a small baby panther sleeping peacefully next to its mother standing tall to ward off any harm from its little one—protecting and loving like a mother should.

"That's a baby panther, Courtney. It's adorable."

Courtney turned to me and smiled from ear to ear; a giggle escaped her lips. She grabbed my hand and tugged me in another direction.

I stood, and we walked hand in hand through the crowds of parents and happy children.

She guided me to the next area. She released my grip and ran.

I quickened my steps to keep pace with her, but I lost sight of her among the busy bodies. My heart fell into my stomach as I pushed past people to see where Courtney had run off to. Relieved, I spotted her twenty feet in front of me. Her face was pressed against the dirty glass as she admired the massive trees, and I shuddered at the sight of so many germs.

"Mommy, Mommy, come look!" She giggled as she bounced on her feet and pointed at the monkeys swinging from limb to limb making lots of chatter amongst themselves.

I loved her laugh. I wanted to bottle it up and save it forever. It was adorable, but I was sure every mother thought their child had the most adorable laugh. I eyed her longingly and wondered how I had created such a beautiful little girl. I smiled.

Her bleach-blond hair glistened in the sun, hanging just below her shoulders with loose curls. I hadn't cut her hair yet; I couldn't bear the thought of cutting those adorable curls. Her skin was brushed with just a touch of tan from playing in the sun this summer, and she had big crystal-blue eyes that glimmered with excitement. I couldn't take my eyes off her as her laughter echoed in my head. I had never been happier.

A dark, glooming shadow rolled over the zoo. I looked up as a droplet of rain hit my forehead, and I blinked. The sky opened and the heavens poured. I gasped. I looked down at Courtney, but she wasn't there. I panicked, my breath catching in my throat. I frantically scanned the people around me, but Courtney was nowhere in sight.

"Courtney! Court-ney!" My voice cracked.

The anxiety built and twisted my insides. My breath quickened, and my heart hammered in my chest as I fought the urge to cry. Desperate, I pushed through the crowd of buzzing people and accidently knocked over a small child who started to cry. But I couldn't look back. I kept going, running faster. The ground beneath me shifted, and my head felt fuzzy and full of clouds. The world spun.

"*Courtney!*" I bellowed a deafening scream.

Everyone turned to stare blankly at me.

A suffocating silence filled the air around me. Confused, I spun to stare at the crowd of adults and children standing expressionless with emptiness behind their gazes. The silence was eerie and sent chills up my spine. I stepped backward and trip over something. Stumbling backward, I tried to catch my balance but hit my head hard, cracking on the pavement, and everything turned black.

***

I awoke abruptly, panicked and drenched in sweat. I sat upright and peeled the sheets off me, trying to catch my breath. It had just been a dream—a wonderful, delightful dream that had turned quickly into a terrible nightmare.

I slid from bed and shuffled into the bathroom. Clenching the sides of the sink for balance, I stared blankly at the reflection in the mirror. The blood had run out of my face, and the lack of sleep was apparent. My eyes were hollow—the life sucked right out of them.

I couldn't keep doing this to myself.

I couldn't live like this any longer.

I couldn't even forget for just a moment while I slept.

The guilt, pain, and suffering was unbearable. I wanted to be with my little girl again. I grabbed the bottle of Xanax from the medicine cabinet. My hands trembled as I twisted and turned the cap. I peered inside, the pills staring back at me. How easy it would be to just end this all for good. I brought the bottle to my quivering lips and tilted back my head as the pills slid in my mouth. I turned the facet; the water filled the cup, and I swallowed hard. Glaring at my pathetic reflection, at the stranger behind my eyes, I suddenly felt relieved. A smile crept across my face, and I walked away to lay in bed.

"Courtney, I'll see you soon, baby." My eyes felt heavy, and I closed them tight as I fell blissfully down a dark rabbit hole.

***

I realized I'd made a terrible mistake. I jolted from bed and ran to the bathroom. I opened the toilet lid and knelt in front of it, shoving my finger down my throat as I gagged. I tried harder; this time my stomach convulsed. Beads of sweat formed on my forehead and the nape of my neck. I needed them out—all of them.

Birthday

I glanced out the window across the room and watched a squirrel scurry up the tree trunk and run across a branch before it disappeared.

"Is something bothering you, Angel?"

I shifted my gaze from the window to her then to the floor, where I stopped and stared for a while, silently trying to gather my composure before I spoke and feeling the hard lump form in my throat. I sniffled, wiping the end of my sleeve across my nose.

"It would've been Courtney's twelfth birthday today," I replied in almost a whisper. I covered my face with my hands, tears streaming down my cheeks.

Jen scooted closer to me, rubbing my back. She didn't say a word, but, when I looked up at her, her eyes were full of tears. If she blinked, they'd roll down her cheeks, but I could tell she was trying to fight them back. I wasn't sure why, maybe to be strong for me. When someone else would start to cry, it would make me cry even harder. She probably didn't want to make this any harder on me than it already was.

I dropped my hands to my lap, and she put her hand on mine—a reassuring touch. Sometimes body language expressed more than words. Jen was a very sweet and caring person. I knew, at this very moment, she'd love to take away all my pain and absorb it into her, so I didn't have to hurt anymore.

She gave me a sad smile.

"I know I haven't shared much with you about her death, because I feel like if I don't talk about it, it will be easier. But it doesn't get any easier. I think about her all the time, how I didn't protect her. I was her mother. Why did I stay with him? It's all my fault." I paused, took a deep breath and exhaled. "I wish I'd never met him. I wish I could take it all back. I wish I could have my Courtney back." I sobbed uncontrollably, my body heaving up and down.

Jen wrapped her arms around me and didn't let go for several minutes.

I cried into her shoulder. It felt good to let it out. The hurt and pain had been eaten me alive. I raised my head to look into her blue eyes. "Do you know what hurts the most?"

Jen shook her head.

"That he got away with murder. It's just not fair. He gets to continue with his life, like nothing ever happened. I don't ever get to see her beautiful smile again or hear her infectious laughter. I'll never touch her again or braid her long, silky blond hair. I'll never read her another bedtime story or ever get the chance to teach her how to ride a bike. All I have left of her are memories. I'll miss out on everything—her birthdays, the first day of school, watching her open all her gifts on Christmas morning, everything." I lowered my head and cried even harder.

We sat in silence for a while.

"Maybe you can start over? Find a good man, start a family together? You deserve to be happy," Jen said softly, her cheeks wet.

"I don't know if I can ever trust a man again. What if he turns out to be a monster just like Jake?"

"Not every man will be Jake, Angel. Good men are out there who will love you, who won't break you down, like Jake did. He will love every inch of you and build you up instead of tearing you down. Someone who will help you get through these terrible times. Someone who will sit and listen to your deepest thoughts, someone who you can trust with every part of your soul. You must let yourself trust again. It's the only way you can move on and be happy again."

I just nodded through the tears. But she was right. Not every man was like Jake. I needed to learn to trust again, I just didn't know how. I forced a smile, and Jen hugged me again.

"Thank you, Jen. It means a lot. You're a great friend. I don't know what I would do without you." I paused. "I think I'll jump in the shower and clear my head, if that's okay with you?"

"Yeah, of course." Jen smiled weakly. "I just want you to know I'll always be here for you no matter what. If you need someone to talk to, even if it's three o'clock in the morning, you call me. I don't care what time it is. You hear me?"

I nodded. "Thank you, Jen. You're an amazing friend."

Jen stood, smiled and left.

I slouched my shoulders and sighed. I realized I hadn't heard the door close behind her. A feeling of loneliness washed over me, not realizing that would be the last time I would ever see or hear from Jen again.

I grabbed the bottle of Jack Daniels I had stored in the back of the kitchen sink and poured a shot. I propped my elbows on the counter and stared blankly through the copper-colored liquor for a long while then poured the liquor down the drain and went to the shower. I felt proud of myself for fighting the urge, hoping a long, hot shower would wash away all these horrible thoughts that kept infesting my frail mind.

After thirty minutes of crying in the shower, I towel dried and threw on some warm clothes. I knelt at the end of my bed and buried my face into the blanket, still trying my hardest to fight the urge that kept creeping up on me. I dropped to the floor and hugged my legs. The urge became too overwhelming. I needed to do something to distract my thoughts. The silence in the house was really getting the best of me. I missed her so much. It was breaking my heart into a million pieces. I just wanted the pain to go away.

I got up and went into the kitchen. I set all the ingredients I needed on the counter, grabbed a big mixing bowl and preheated the oven to 350 degrees. I sprayed the cake pan and threw all the ingredients into the bowl and mixed and mixed and mixed some more, staring at nothing. I poured the batter into the pan and opened the oven door, scalding my face from the heat. I set the pan on the rack and closed the oven door. I set the oven timer, sat on the floor and blankly stared for thirty minutes as the tears continued to roll.

Beep. Beep. Beep. The sound startled me from my trance. I removed the pan from the oven and set it on a cooling rack. I got impatient waiting for it to cool, so I licked the spoon of buttercream frosting I had prepared. Yum. Silky and sweet. Courtney would love this. A smile crept across my face.

I began to frost the cake, but the cake was still warm, and it crumbled. Frustrated, I scooped a big dollop of frosting onto the spatula and slapped it on as the cake continued to fall apart. In desperation, I retrieved twelve candles from the cabinet and, in between tears, stuck them in the appalling-looking chocolate cake and carried it into the dining room, singing between sobs, "*Happy birthday to you. Happy birthday to you ...*" I looked up, but no one was sitting at the other end of the table with a smiling face waiting to blow out her candles.

My eyes burned, and my throat was raw from crying so much today. I halted and laughed hysterically—not a belly laugh from something funny but one full of sadness, tears, and teetering on psychosis.

How badly I just wanted to look up and see my daughters face smiling at me and getting excited after every gift she opened. How badly I just wanted to hold her in my arms and tell her how sorry I was for what I did. How badly I wanted to squeeze her so tight and never let her go. But I couldn't have that ever again.

My maniacal laughter turned quickly into anger. I threw the cake across the room in a rage and watched as it stuck to the wall and slid to the floor in a blob of sticky crumbs. I fell to the floor and brought my knees to my chest and hug my knees, rocking back and forth.

I couldn't take this any longer. I stood, pulled down my shirt and returned to the kitchen. I poured a shot of whiskey into my drinking glass, tilted back my head, downed the shot, slammed it onto the counter and poured another. The delicious liquor sliding down my throat and warming my belly had never felt so good.

10ᵀᴴ ANNIVERSARY
(THEN)

"Angel, do you know why you're here?" Dr. Melville asked while peering over the rim of her glasses.

"Of course."

"Then, why are you here?"

"I'm confused …"

"With your state of mind, I want to hear from you why you think you're here."

"Well, that's a dumb question." I nervously shifted my weight in the seat. I didn't know what she was trying to get at.

"Please answer the question." Dr. Melville slightly tilted her head to the side, gazing at me with an expression I couldn't read.

"Well …" I crossed my left leg over the right and intertwined my fingers in my lap. I rubbed my thumb into the palm of the opposite hand in a circular motion.

Dr. Melville squinted at my foot unconsciously bouncing side to side and sighed heavily.

I rubbed the back of my neck. "I-I tried to harm myself after Courtney died." I studied my hands.

"How did you harm yourself?"

I tried to read her expression. I couldn't tell if she was concerned, annoyed, or frustrated with me.

Dr. Melville raised an eyebrow behind her tiny rimmed glasses while patiently waiting for my response, looking more like a librarian than a psychiatrist. She cleared her throat and shifted her weight.

"I swallowed a bunch of pills."

"Have you tried to harm yourself since then?"

"Not for a couple years. But yes, a few times since being here." Ashamed, I lifted my sleeve to expose the scar that ran above my wrist. It was a thick, jagged white scar now. I must've cut it deep.

"You lost a lot of blood that day."

"I don't remember much of that day."

"You were in and out of consciousness. We thought we had lost you."

I didn't know what to say. I frowned and looked down at my lap then back at her again.

"Do you know how long you've been in here?"

I hesitated, uncertain of the answer. "A few years." I shrugged.

"It's your ten-year anniversary today. You've been institutionalized at this facility for ten long years." Dr. Melville thumbed through her notes. "That's why we're here. I have to tell the judge today if you're safe to leave this place to live on your own and if you're a threat to yourself or anyone else." She paused, looking at me hard, squinting and studying me. "Angel. Do you think you're a harm to yourself or anyone else?"

"Of course not." I shook my head.

"How often do you think about ending your life?"

"I don't." I hesitated. "Not anymore."

"Where will you live when you leave here?"

"My house."

"Who's been taking care of it for the last ten years?"

"My sister."

"The one who comes and visits you once a week?"

"Yes."

"Have you been writing in your journal?"

"Almost every day."

"Did you want to bring it home with you?"

I sat and contemplated for a while. If I wanted to survive on my own, it was probably best if I stayed as far away from the journal as possible. I didn't want to be reminded of the dark thoughts I'd had and still have. But I wasn't about to tell the doctor that; I'd never leave this place. "Could you hang onto it for me?"

"I will, but, at some point, you'll have to read it again. Angel, you need to know the truth of why you've been here for ten years. I hope you realize a suicide attempt wouldn't keep you locked up in here for ten years. You realize that, right?"

"Yeah, of course." But really, I was only telling her what she wanted to hear at this point. I'd tried hurting myself many times while being here. I rubbed my skull and felt the dent. I was so screwed up. I just smiled and nodded.

"I think Mary should stay with you for a couple weeks, until you get used to living on your own again. This is a big step and transition for you. I don't want you pedaling backward or end up back in here again. Okay?"

"Yeah of course." I smiled. "Mary will stay with me for a couple weeks."

"Okay. I'll write up a report for the judge, and, if he agrees with your release, you may be going home as soon as tomorrow." Dr. Melville grinned from ear to ear, stood and approached me. "Now, give me a hug."

I rose and gave her a long hug. "Thank you, Dr. Melville … for everything."

She pulled away and quickly wiped the tear that had escaped from her wet eyes. "Make me proud, Angel," she said with a shaky voice.

"I will." I gave her a big smile and walked away.

"Angel."

"Yeah?" I turned around.

"I'll stop by your room later for your journal. And you call me anytime, if you need anything. And I mean anything. Here's my personal phone number." She scratched numbers on a piece of paper and handed it to me. "I don't care what time of the day or night it is. You can call me. I'm only a phone call away."

"Thank you."

COLD CASE
(NOW)

I walked to the mailbox, grabbed the mail and brought it inside. I set it on the counter. The newspaper was folded in half, and the photo on the front page caught my attention. Picking it up, I unfolded it.

A Forty-Year Cold Case Solved!

> *Forty years ago, an entire family went missing. A county-wide search went on for months, searching the woods and nearby lakes without a clue or any evidence. The family of five had seemed to just disappear without a trace. After months with no leads, it became a cold-case file, buried and almost forgotten, until new evidence came to light, and the detective unit reopened the case. A man claimed that his cellmate, Scott E. Jacobson, in the Sioux Falls State Penitentiary had admitted to murdering a family, cutting them into tiny pieces and setting their remains on fire. Jacob-*

son, who was consumed with guilt and hadn't slept in weeks, said his victims' ghosts were haunting him. He felt the only way to make them go away was to confess to the murders. He's not sure what triggered their ghostly appearances after all these years, but that something or someone must have disturbed the house that had been forgotten many years ago.

I gasped when I turned the page. It was a picture of the abandoned house we had found deep in the woods. I continued to read.

With the advanced technology we didn't have forty years ago, criminal investigators found blood matching the five victims that had seeped into the floorboard cracks in their abandoned house. A rock-formed pit sat a hundred feet from the house, but law enforcement couldn't collect any evidence. State officials believe that is where Scott E. Jacobson had burned their remains after desecrating them. He refused to tell authorities his motive for killing the family. Scott E. Jacobson plead guilty to five counts of murder in the first degree and will serve 5 life sentences without a chance of parole. Justice has finally been served.

I closed the newspaper and stared off in disbelief. Me, Matthew, and Michael had been in that very house many years ago as children. It gave me the creeps, thinking we had walked through a house where someone had brutally murdered five people. The hair on the back of my neck stood on end. *That poor, poor family. What could they have ever done to deserve that? Those poor children must have been terrified.*

I picked up the phone and dialed Matthew's number.

Ring.

Ring.

Ring.

"*You've reached Matt's phone. Leave a message.*" *Beeeeeeeep.*

"Matthew. It's Angel. Call me. It's important." *Click.*

I stood and paced the room, biting my nails. *Had Matthew and Michael returned to the house and done something to disturb it? Matthew better call me back soon, or I'll drive myself crazy.*

***

Two hours had passed, and my phone finally. I impatiently answered after the first ring.

"Angel, it's Matt. I just got your message. What's going on?' Michael asked with concern.

"Did you see the front page of the paper?"

"Or course, who hasn't? Everyone's talking about it at the office."

"Did you or Matthew go back there recently?" There was a long pause. "Matthew? Are you still there?"

"Yeaaahhh …?"

"Well, did you?"

Matthew cleared his throat. "We … um …. wanted to go back after all these years and try something."

"Try what?"

"We took a Ouija board—"

"You what?"

"I know. I know. It was stupid."

"Well, apparently you disrupted the family who died there."

"How were we supposed to know a family was murdered there?"

"Did anything happen while you were there?"

"Oh yeah. Some crazy, fucked-up shit!"

"Like what?"

There was another long pause. "A loud crash startled us. Then all the cabinets and doors opened and slammed shut repeatedly. It was like the house had come alive. It shook like an earthquake. We thought we would fall through the damn floorboards. We ran out of there, screaming like little girls."

"Oh. My. God."

"Yeah, I know. It was some crazy shit!"

"But hey, look at the bright side. Good came out of it. The guy who brutally murdered that family finally came forward and confessed."

"True."

"Guess you won't be playing with any Ouija boards anytime soon." I laughed.

"Nope. We burned it. I vowed never to touch one of them ever again. I pissed my pants I was so scared."

We both laughed.

"But hey, Angel?"

"Yeah?"

"It was nice hearing from you. But I must get back to work. Don't be a stranger. We'll have to get together some time."

"Yeah. Sure. Bye, Michael."

"Bye."

Click.

I plopped onto the couch, laid back and stared at the ceiling. What had they been thinking, bringing a Ouija board into that creepy old house? Gave me the creeps just thinking about it. I couldn't believe I had walked through a house where someone had murdered an entire family—and not just murdered but cut into tiny pieces and burned. Chills ran down my spine.

The Farmhouse

The throbbing in my skull was so intense it felt like I had gotten beat in the head with a hammer too many times. But I don't remember what happened or how I got here. I winced as I touched my head. I blinked hard a few times, trying to focus on my surroundings. Everything was so fuzzy and dull looking, and the taste of old pennies lingered in my mouth.

What happened?

I pushed myself off the filthy hardwood floors covered in years of neglect, my arms weak and trembling. A sharp pain shot up them as I cried out in pain. I slowly sat upright and surveyed the room, my head spinning. The smell of mold and dust invaded my throat and nose, causing me to cough. I raised my hand to my mouth but quickly pulled it away when I noticed some sort of black substance covered it. I shuddered, wiping it on my pants.

The room was dark and damp and covered in cobwebs and dust. It smelled old and dirty. I scrunched my face in disgust. Scanning the room, something familiar caught my attention—a picture hanging on the wall.

Where have I seen this before?

I sat and wracked my brain for the slightest remembrance. I stood up slowly and approached it. I wiped away the years of dust with a couple strokes. It was an old black and white photo. A family—a mother, father, and three children; two boys and a girl—stood on a farmhouse porch with such serious expressions. I remembered this picture. I looked a little closer. I swore the woman looked just like Jennifer. Maybe it was her grandmother. She never told me about her family. To be honest, I really didn't know much about Jen. I should've asked more questions, pried a little. Instead, I was selfish, more worried about myself and my own problems than to ask Jen about hers. I was a terrible friend. I didn't deserve her friendship.

Where am I?

Confused, I step backward and spin around the room.

I've been here before.

I gasped, my eyes wide, and ran toward the door. I pushed through it as a loud creak echoes and bounces off the empty walls. I stepped outside just as my foot went through a rotted porch board. I screamed in pain as the jagged board sliced my shin. I caught my fall with both hands, sending pain rippling through my body. I grasped the broken board, moving it back and forth to loosen it before ripping it out, which wasn't very difficult, since it disintegrated in my hands. I pulled out my leg and stared in horror at the blood seeping from the gash and cringed.

I stumbled off the porch and stared at the house, the one from the picture. And all the memories came rushing back—the day as a kid I had stumbled out here after Matthew and Michael had told me they had found it in the woods and had made me pinky promise not to say anything to Grandpa about it. I remembered them hiding in the closet in one of the rooms and had jumped out to scare the shit out of me. I thought I had peed my pants that day, they had scared me so bad.

I remembered being drawn to this place, like I had been here before. It was so weird. I still couldn't believe I had come here on my own when I was a kid, I had been such a scaredy-cat. And now, after reading the newspaper about that poor family being murdered here, that was horrible! How had I ended up here? Just more empty holes in my memory. I didn't remember anything that had led me to this point, just waking up on the filthy floor of the abandoned farmhouse where a murdered had cut an entire family into little pieces and burned them. The thought sent shivers down my spine, and the hair on my arms stood on end.

An overwhelming feeling of sadness ran through my veins as I stared at the farmhouse as tears welled in my eyes. I didn't ever want their family to be forgotten. I carefully climbed the porch steps and reentered the creepy house. I took down the creepy picture of the family and tucked it under my arm just as a memory flashed in front of my eyes—*a doll*. I turned to the room at the back of the house as the boards under my feet creaked and moaned with my every step. I carefully walked around, scanning every corner of the room. I noticed a small rocking chair near the back of the room and waited for something to jump out and scare me like last time. I snatched the doll with trembling hands and ran from the house as fast as I could, slamming the front door behind me.

I was breathing heavy now, scared out of my mind. I crouched over, my hands resting on my knees as my heart hammered. I peeked at the abandoned farmhouse. As creepy as it was, I felt sad it has been forgotten just like the family who used to live here.

After catching my breath, I stood, stretched out my back and raised the doll to eye level. Years of thick dust covered the doll. Its eyes were missing, like a mouse or another hungry animal had eaten them. Its hair had been cut very uneven, adding to its creepiness. A long dress—or what was left of one—hung to its feet, but, with all the years of neglect, I couldn't tell its color under all the dirt and dust.

I turned the doll over and gasped, dropping it to the ground. The hole where the eyes should've been were bleeding. I picked it up, my heart racing, but, when I turned it over, there was no blood. I must have imagined it. I shrugged. It just needs a little TLC. It'll be back to new with just a little soap and water. I smiled.

Ouch. The frame pinched me. I grabbed it from under my left arm and tucked it under my right arm, hoping it would be more comfortable this way. I inspected my dirty hands and shook my head, but there was no use wiping them; they'd just get dirty again.

I took one last gander at the sad farmhouse hunched over like a ghostly silhouette. The windows were boarded up, moss covered the caved-in roof, and a rotted porch and siding were suffocating underneath ivy crawling up like skeleton fingers waiting to pull it underground and bury it forever, as if it never had existed.

Dr Melville
(Then)

I had just finished my session with Dr. Melville. She wanted me to keep a journal while I was in here. I wasn't sure if it would do any good, but I guess there was not much else for me to do here except stare at the walls. At first, I didn't like her. I didn't like being in here. I hated everyone and everything. I just wanted to turn to dust and disappear and never return to this nightmare.

We had sat for many sessions without saying a word. I didn't want to talk to anyone. If I talked about it, it wouldn't change anything. It wouldn't bring back my precious Courtney. I was a heartless monster.

I knew the second I laid eyes on my baby for the first time that something was wrong with me. I had plead guilty. I knew what I had done. I had drowned my daughter in the bathtub. I couldn't deal with all the crying. She cried *all* the time. I had tried everything to comfort her, but nothing made her stop. It drove me insane. Her cries would rattle inside my skull louder and louder. I would pull clumps of hair from my head. I would cry myself to sleep almost every night. I slept very little and hardly ate.

I told myself lies to keep myself sane in here, because the truth hurt so much worse. If I told myself I loved her more than life itself, it would tear me apart.

So, to survive in here, I started to hate her and how she had ruined everything. She must have sensed my hatred, and that's why she cried all the time; I didn't love her like I should've. They say babies can sense your mood. I think they're right. I had told myself I never wanted to get pregnant; it just happened. Jake had been so happy, but all I could think about was how fat I would get and how a baby would ruin my body. I never wanted kids. I think they're ungrateful pukes. All they do is shit their pants, puke and cry all the time. You lose sleep and all your freedom. They're like vultures; they eat every piece of you until nothing's left.

So, I began to hate her, and I began to hate Jake. I told myself lies about him too. Because he had left me. He had left me alone. He had let me rot in here, but I don't blame him.

She asked me how I was dealing with being in here. I shrugged, told her the book selection here was terrible. I just wanted to read. Reading was my only escape from reality, the only way I could survive in this place. She offered to bring me some of her favorite books from home. I told her anything would be better than these. I took the book I had forced myself to read because there was nothing better and chucked it across the room.

The day she brought me books was when I began to like her and open up to her. Eventually, I told her everything—my innermost thoughts and feelings. She became my best friend. I looked forward to our sessions. It gave me someone to talk to instead of talking to myself, because I was going a little coo-coo in here. When you spend too much time alone, away from people, away from the things you love, you start to dwindle into nothing. Your thoughts drift to dark places. You dream of ways to hurt yourself and end it all. It's a hard pill to swallow, being institutionalized for killing your child. But no one judges you here. We're all crazy and have a screw loose upstairs.

I sometimes wonder if I had gone to prison instead of being committed here, if I could've pulled myself together and picked up all the pieces. At least there I wouldn't have been in lockdown 24/7. At least there I could've mingled with other inmates, played cards, and went outside, even if it's inside a cage. Here we are confided to four walls, no window, no one to talk to except ourselves, and that would make anyone go insane. But I suppose they think we already are insane, so what's the difference?

I learned in our session today that she had read through my files with Dr. Kurtenbach. He had treated me for postpartum depression shortly after I had Courtney. I was having a hard time adjusting to being a mom. I was severely depressed and didn't understand why I wanted nothing to do with my daughter. Everyone says they fall in love with their child the first time they lay eyes on them, but I never experienced that. I looked down at her and felt *nothing*. That was when I knew something was very wrong with me. How could I not love this precious tiny human being? She looked up at me, and I'm sure any mother's heart would melt but not mine.

I thought she looked like an alien. Her head and eyes were too big for her body. I thought maybe she would grow on me, but the complete opposite happened. This big space existed between us that kept growing bigger and bigger. I think she felt it too, even though she was just a baby, because all she did was cry. Cried about everything. She needed my affection, my attention, to be held, to be cuddled. But I couldn't deal with her and all the awkwardness.

I thought by being a mother something magical would happen, but instead, I wished I could return her to the hospital and runaway. Or shove her back inside me, and somehow, she'd just disappear.

I started drinking a lot. I became a closet drinker. I despised Jake for being a raging alcoholic, but it was the only way I could cope. I laid her down in her crib, shut the door and walked away as she wailed. I would pour a drink—vodka usually, since it had no scent—and curl up and cry. But I could still hear her muffled cries, so I would turn up the music to drown her out.

But that's not what really happened. The only truth was the drinking. I tried everything. I tried to rock her, cuddle her, give her a warm bath, put on a clean diaper and a clean change of clothes. I would nurse her and sing her lullabies, but nothing worked; her cries would grow louder. I depended on the alcohol to keep me sane, to deal with the crying. But it didn't help; it made me more agitated. I would lose my patience with her. I should've never started to drink.

It was evil.
It made me evil.

This place is making me go crazy. I can't remember what was real and what was lies anymore. It's all blending together like watercolors on a canvas. The watercolors are the truth and lies mixed together, and the canvas is my tragic life. Maybe there's some truth to my lies. All I know is I couldn't deal with the truth anymore; it shred my heart into tiny slivers then burned to dust.

The lies made it easier. Soon the lies will become the truth, and I won't know the difference. But that was the point, wasn't it?

My daughter is dead, and my husband left me here to rot, locked up in this hellhole. I wish my daughter was alive. I wish we were happy again. I wish I'd wake up from this terrible nightmare and everything would return to the way it was. If only I could turn back time and start over.

Doesn't everyone deserve a second chance? But I don't get one. I can't take back what I did. My punishment is living with the pain, heartache, and guilt as it slowly eats me alive like maggots. I wish the world would show me some mercy. I was a good mother; I tried. I would never hurt my little girl.

My life is a tragic mercy. My punishment. My hell. And I deserve every bit of it. I deserve to rot in this hell. I don't deserve mercy. I don't deserve anything.

THE TRUTH ABOUT JEN

Had I gone mad? Everything I thought was real was just a figment of my imagination. Jennifer Drown had never existed. At least, that's what my therapist told me. She said someone just doesn't disappear into the night, as I had claimed. She was an imaginary friend I had devised in my head when I was at my lowest and loneliness point of my pathetic life. Well, she didn't call me pathetic, I did.

Dr. Melville has a friend who works in a police department who did a search on Jennifer Drown. The only ones who popped up in their records were much younger or much older and lived in different states. The only one from this area had died forty years ago, disappeared without a trace. That Jennifer Drown was the mother and wife of the five people who were murdered forty years ago. I gasped. That can't be true. There's no way. I saw her. I talked to her. She was my best friend.

I remember the day she moved into town and the moving truck and all the times we sat and talked for hours. But what did I really know about her? Nothing, really. She sat and listened. I always thought she was a good listener. She didn't say much, just stayed quiet and let me spill my guts. And best of all, she never judged me even after everything I told her. Which was more comforting than she knew. She was an amazing friend.

I would make her dinner. She had brought me lasagna. She had knocked on my door in middle of the storm and stayed with me for the night, and we had drunk wine and talked all night. But now that I think about it, why hadn't she brought her boyfriend if they had lost power and needed to stay warm? Only she had come. Where had Jen moved here from? She would never talk about friends and family. No one would come and visited, except me.

I had to know for myself if it was true. I walked to Jen's house and knocked on the door, but no one answered. I stepped backward and took in my surroundings. The house was rundown, looked like it hadn't been lived in for decades. The paint was peeling. The roof shingles were rotted. Plants grew in the gutters, and the windows were boarded up. This couldn't be! I remember going into this house, having dinner with Jen and her boyfriend. I remember everything. Or had I made it all up? My mind has been deteriorating for as long as I can remember.

I must recall all the times she had stopped over. It was like she knew when I was at my lowest. I would hear a knock on the door, and Jen would always be there with a smiling face to make things all better. I thought it was because we had a strong connection, like she could sense when I needed her most. But she was just a figment of my imagination, an imaginary friend who never existed. A ghost. How twisted and sick was I? I'd never felt so alone and scared. Scared of my own mind and what else it was capable of making up.

My stomach twisted into knots, and I felt lightheaded. I grabbed the counter for balance. I picked up the closest thing to me—a glass of wine—and chucked it across the room, and it shattered into pieces. I screamed at the top of my lungs until I ran out of breath. It felt good to scream.

I stared at the red poison on the wall and the broken pieces. I collapsed to the floor and sobbed, hugging my legs as I rocked back and forth. I felt my grip on sanity evaporate and disappear into the air.

A Splintered Mind

It happened slowly. Forgetting my car keys when I walked out the door. Forgetting a doctor's appointment. Forgetting a birthday. No biggie. I excused it as stress, but that was only the beginning. I forgot much more important things over time. I forgot to book the hotel for our trip. We spent all day driving. We were exhausted when we reached the hotel, and it was completely booked. But that wasn't the worst part; every hotel within a thirty mile radius was completely booked for a popular event happening in town that weekend. We ended up sleeping in the car that night. I hardly slept; I couldn't get comfortable. No one could.

Then I forgot to pay bills. Our electricity was shut off and then our water. I overdrew our account many times, costing us thousands of dollars in overdraft fees. When Courtney was a baby, I forgot her in the car while I was grocery shopping. Thank God it wasn't freezing cold or smoldering hot outside. I felt terrible. How could a mother forget her baby?

I even forgot to turn off the gas burner on the stove one day. Thank goodness I wasn't the only one in the house; we could have gone to bed and never woke up again. This was getting serious, and I was putting other people lives in jeopardy.

I was eventually diagnosed with early onset Alzheimer's disease at the age of forty-two. At first, Mary would visit every day to check on me. Once she realized how bad I was getting, she stayed with me for a while. But eventually, I was too much for her to handle; I needed twenty-four-hour care. I wondered off one day while she was in the shower. She spent all day looking for me. She finally found me at dusk on a deserted road miles from my house. When she approached me, I didn't even know who she was. Just like what had happened to my grandmother.

That week, I moved into a nursing home. Mary visited me often in the beginning, but over time, her visits became less and less. I don't blame her. I don't know what I would have done if the roles had been reversed. I was in the nursing home for many years, and then one day, Mary visited, rambling about some book she had found in her attic and that a curse had been haunting our family for a century that had claimed the lives of many, as well as was the culprit of the endless tragedies our family had to endure throughout the years. She went on to claim I was the only person who could break this curse, that I was the angel born into our family. None of this made any sense, but later that night, Mary and her grandson, Trevor, snuck me into the woods where I recited a spell and broke a terrible, deadly curse.

Once I had broken the curse, things returned to normal, as if I had finally lifted this dark cloud that had been hovering over our family for a century and now our family was spared from this evil curse—the curse of Jack the Ripper, our great-great-great grandfather.

I regained my memory but at what cost? The memories I had buried deep in the darkest corners of my mind slowly returned. The memories of the mental institution where I had spent ten years of my life. The memories of my precious Courtney. The memories of Jake. The lies I had been telling myself for so many years were being exposed for its whole truth. My splintered mind was slowly healing, or was it? I felt like I was living in a bubble—a bubble to protect me from my mind and from the truth—because I couldn't live with the truth.

The truth of what I had done.

The truth that would cost me my life.

The truth that would seal the deal of my fate.

A curse we all thought I had broken many years ago crept back into our lives. Bad blood was never forgiven. Bad blood would continue to run through our veins. It all came down to the ugly truth.

The day someone knocked on my door changed everything. And that's when I knew it had to all come to an end.

ISABELLA

I couldn't shake the feeling; it was dominating the room and consuming my soul. A deep shiver ran through me. The lack of sleep had my head full of fuzz and the air heavy. My body stiffened.

I imagined him lying in bed, laughing. Laughing at the fact he had gotten away with murder, that he had broken me and destroyed my life. And how I couldn't go a day without thinking of him—hating him—my thoughts obsessive.

I saw him as if he was right in front of me, taunting me, with his evil laughter and sinister intensions.

Laughing at how he destroyed me so easily.

Laughing until he falls asleep.

Laughing with a psychotic smile across his face until he sleeps like a baby with not a care in the world.

I clenched my fists and gritted my teeth. I leapt into the bed and pounded the pillow where his head would be. I squeezed my eyes tight and punched harder and faster, expelling all my frustration as I sobbed between each heart-wrenching blow. When all my energy was gone, I collapsed on the bed and covered my face with my pillow and screamed. I screamed so loud I'm sure I'd woken the entire sleeping town. I clenched the sheets in my fists and fought with them, kicking and screaming.

As quickly as my tantrum started, it stopped. I laid motionless in bed as the silence consumed me, staring at the ceiling and panting. The room was caving in on me, becoming smaller and suffocating me.

A loud rap on the front door startled me. I shuffled down the stairs, rolling my head from side to side as it snapped, cracked, and popped. I turned the bolt lock and opened the door.

A young lady stood before me, her hood pulled over her head, and she was drenched from the rain. She looked nervous. She kept looking from side to side as if she didn't want to be seen.

"Can I help you?"

"C-Can I come in?"

"Umm … sure." I stepped aside, so she could come in from the rain.

She removed her hood and shuddered. "I'm sure you don't recognize me. I've cut my hair short and dyed it black."

"You're right. I don't know who you are."

"I visited you a few years ago with your sister, Mary. I'm Isabella. Trevor was my dad, Mary's grandson."

My eyes widened. "I vaguely remember, but you look much different. Is everything okay?"

"No."

Isabella pulled back the curtain just enough to peek through it. She seemed paranoid and was making me feel uncomfortable.

Something wasn't right, I could feel it. "Can I do anything?"

"Can I stay here for a while?"

"Sure. Stay as long as you need, but you're scaring me. If you're staying here, you need to tell me what's happening."

"It's a long story. Do you mind if I take a hot shower? I haven't showered in days.

"Yeah, of course." I forced a smile. "It looks like you haven't slept much either."

"I haven't. Is it *that* obvious?" She looked at her feet.

I nodded then shrugged.

"I should grab my bag. I left it on the porch outside." She stepped outside for a minute while the door was ajar. She returned with a big duffle bag slung over her shoulder then dropped it to the floor with a loud thud. "It's heavy," she said a little out of breath.

"How did you get here?"

"I took the train to Minneapolis, caught a ride with someone to Sioux Falls. Then hitchhiked the rest of the way."

"Hitchhiking is dangerous."

"I can protect myself. They should be scared of me."

"Why would you say such a thing?"

"Long story. I'll tell you later. Can I take that shower now?"

"Sure. It's upstairs. You can put your things in the guest bedroom at the end of the hallway to your left. The bathroom is at the top of the stairs."

"Thanks." Isabella smiled, gave me an awkward hug then headed for the stairs.

***

Isabella was upstairs for a couple hours. I suppose she needed a long shower then laid down for a while. I left her alone. I tried to wrap my head around all this, tried to figure out how Mary's great-grandchild had managed to arrive on my doorstep and was now staying with me for a while. I suppose company would be nice. I don't know much about Mary's grandson or his child. This would be the perfect chance to get to know her. She seemed nice but on edge. Something was definitely off about her. And why would she imply strangers should fear her more than she would fear them? Made no sense. She looked to be in her twenties maybe. Still so young.

I opened the fridge and scanned the contents. I did the same with the pantry. Isabella must be hungry. I didn't have much; it was usually just me here. I hadn't been to a grocery store in a couple weeks. My pantry and fridge were pretty much bare. I found a box of noodles and a jar of homemade sauce I had canned a couple years ago. Looked like we were having spaghetti. I glanced at the clock, realizing it was much too early for a drink, but I made one anyways to take the edge off.

I turned off the stove and covered the pots with lids to keep them warm for when Isabella decided to come downstairs and join me. I was curious to know what had brought her halfway across the country to my house. She definitely didn't want to discuss it. I hoped she wasn't in any trouble.

I approached the living room, drink in hand. I gave it a gentle swirl as the ice clanged on the side and sipped. I set it on the coffee table, and something startled me, almost making me spill my drink.

"Jesus Christ. You scared me," I said, my voice caught in my throat.

"Sorry about that. I'm pretty quiet. Most the time you won't even know I'm here. I'm really sorry for intruding on you like this. I know I was the last person you expected to see on your doorstep." She sat next to me and looked at her folded her hands in her lap, avoiding eye contact.

"Is everything okay, sweetie?"

"I really don't want to talk about it right now, if that's alright with you?"

"Sure, of course." I smiled. "Are you hungry?"

"Starved. I can't remember the last time I ate. It was a couple days ago, I think."

"I don't have much. I wasn't expecting company."

"It's okay. I didn't expect you to cook me a five-course meal or anything." She chuckled, finally making eye contact with me. Her eyes were a beautiful ice blue. She had a very nice smile too; it reminded me of Mary's.

"I made spaghetti. I know it's early, but it's all I had. If I knew you were coming, I would have made some eggs and toast."

"Spaghetti is perfect." She smiled. "I would probably eat a dead squirrel if you had any of those hanging around." She tilted back her head and laughed.

I laughed with her. It felt good to laugh. I hadn't laughed in a long time. I felt like I didn't deserve to be happy. My life was so fucked, and I didn't know how to un-fuck it. And then I woke up, and Mary's great-granddaughter was on my front doorstep. How much weirder could this get?

We sat at the dining room table, the first time I'd sat at it to eat a meal in years. I didn't know why I hadn't sat at it more often; it was absolutely beautiful and had cost me a fortune. Its dark mahogany matched just about everything in this house—the kitchen cabinets, pantry, all the doors and their frames, windowsills, bookcases, coffee table, and baseboards. I loved it!

I pushed the noodles around on my plate, my nerves getting the best of me. But most of all, I was curious as to what Isabella was doing here. I stared at her while she shoveled the food into her mouth like a garbage disposal. I wondered when the last time was she had eaten a meal. She looked sick—nothing but skin and bones. Her face was sunken, and the dark circles did her beautiful eyes no justice; they looked like she hadn't slept in ages.

I had the sudden urge to pour another drink, but I needed to pace myself this early in the day. It wasn't even close to noon yet.

"Would you like mine?" I asked, pushing my plate toward Isabella.

"Are you sure? Aren't you hungry?"

"No. I haven't been feeling so well. You eat it. I'll eat something later. I have to run to the store and pick up some groceries. Would you like to come with me?"

She stiffened and paused from eating, staring blankly at the food in front of her. "I can't."

"Why not?"

"Like I said before, it's a long story. But I can't be seen in public."

A terrible feeling rushed through me. My stomach clenched, and it felt like barbwire twisted and cut my insides. What had she done? I was sure it was nothing compared to what I had done.

Nothing compares.

"I'm going upstairs to lie down. I'm not feeling well. Please make yourself at home." I paused. "Through those doors"—I pointed—"is my study. It's full of books, if they interest you at all. I've got lots of them."

"I love books!" Isabella's eyes lit up.

"Good, that's something we have in common then." I smiled and sauntered to the stairs.

I closed my bedroom door behind me and unlocked the trunk at the foot of my bed. I had found it at an antique shop in mint condition. It too was made of mahogany and not a scratch on it. Had cost me a pretty penny. I opened the lid and removed my journal. I needed to read more. I needed to understand my sick and twisted mind. I needed to know all the things I had buried deep in the dark corners of my splintered mind and wipe away all the cobwebs and dust that had formed there throughout the years.

I sat on my bed, crisscrossed my legs, took a deep breath and opened the first page.

THE TERRIBLE TRUTH

I woke with a terrible headache. My mind cracked like an egg, spidering outward in every direction until one last blow turned it all to mush, and, with just a little heat, it bubbled and boiled and scrambled to pieces.

I had been drinking all night, trying to drown the truth and all the memories that had come flooding back to me like a tidal wave after I had read my journal. All the lies I had been telling myself for so long were finally being exposed. And, all this time, the truth had been hiding like a scared child in the darkest corners of my psyche in a broken and fragile mind.

***

The rain had been coming down in sheets all day. I pulled aside the curtain and looked outside, trying to peer through the blurred and distorted images as the rain violently assaulted the window. An explosive rumble rattled the windows and shook the floor, snapping me into reality as the cries continued from upstairs, ripping through the suffocating air. I squeezed my eyes tight, clenched my jaw and drew a deep breath. I plopped onto the couch, covering my ears while my legs bounced nervously. Then I bellowed a deafening scream so loud my voice cracked, and, just for a second, the crying from upstairs stopped. I flopped to the floor and slammed my fists into the carpet in a violent outrage as pain shot up my arms.

It needs to stop. The crying needs to stop. I can't keep doing this.

I sat upright with my feet under my butt and stared blankly. I covered my face and burst into uncontrollable sobs. My body heaved up and down. I took deep breaths, trying to calm myself, but it didn't help. I pushed myself off the floor and traipsed into the kitchen and poured myself a shot of strong liquor and downed it, feeling the warm liquid trickle down my throat. I slammed the glass on the counter and poured another as the cries from upstairs vibrated in my skull. I sighed heavily and grabbed my hair, wanting to pull out every last strand in clumps. I dropped to the floor and drew my knees to my chest and rocked back and forth on the brink of insanity.

My doctor had told me a few weeks ago that I suffered from postpartum depression, and having a colicky baby probably didn't help. I swore all she did was cry all the time, and it was definitely worse at night. I couldn't deal with it anymore. It was too much, and I felt like I was going insane.

Jake was upstairs passed out, sleeping like a rock. He never got up with the baby; he could sleep through everything. And I resented him for it. I wished I could sleep through her cries, but I wasn't that fortunate. They just echoed and vibrated in my skull until I couldn't take it anymore. Not even the violent rain or thunder drowned out her cries; they just kept getting louder and more frequent. I just wanted to throw her across the room to make it stop. Maybe smother her with a pillow. Anything to make the crying stop. *Anything!*

I needed to stop thinking this way. I loved Courtney; she was my everything. She was so precious and beautiful when she wasn't crying. I loved her smile. She made my heart melt. She was the best thing that had ever happened to me. I'd never loved and hated someone so much.

I decided a hot bath might do me some good. So I climbed the stairs and ran the hot water, staring as it fills the tub. The water drowned out her cries just a little but not enough. I glanced into our bedroom and saw Jake sound asleep. I shook my head in disgust, clenching my jaw and fists. I wanted to crawl into bed and just beat him senseless. It was just not fair. How could he sleep through all the crying?

I closed the door with a slam, trying to wake him, but I knew it wouldn't do any good. I went to Courtney's bedroom and glanced down at her in her crib, my heart racing and palms sweaty. Her face was scrunched and beet read; she looked ridiculous. Nothing was wrong with her. I had fed her before I had laid her down. She'd had a nice bath, clean diaper, and a change of clothes before bed. She just needed to stop. This was absurd. All I saw was red, and I slapped her. She stopped for just a second—I must have startled her—then she started wailing again, this time even louder. I clamped my hands over my ears, fighting the urge to cry.

Snapping into reality, I realized the water was still running. I strode to the bathroom and turned off the water. I nervously paced as the crying continued. I took a deep breath and held it for several seconds, trying to calm my nerves. But it didn't help. She was still crying.

I entered her room and picked her up from the crib and bounced her, rubbing her back. But her body was tense, and she just kicked and screamed. I tried to sing her a lullaby and rock her back to sleep, but she continued to cry. I could feel my blood boiling. The tension hung thick in the air. I held her out and shook her. *Please stop! Please stop!* Tears streamed down my cheeks. I shook her again, but she continued to cry. I stormed to the bathroom, Courtney draped over my shoulder as she screamed loud in my ear.

"*Stop it! Stop it now!*" I yelled.

I held her at arm's length, her face still beet red. I couldn't take it anymore. I leaned over and dipped her body into the tub until her head submerged underwater.

Her eyes widened and stared up at me.

I held her there.

Tiny bubbles formed around her mouth as she screamed, but the room remained silent.

How much I had craved the silence. My body relaxed, and a smile crept across my face. It was finally quiet.

Newspaper Clippings

My nerves were on edge, and I was literally climbing the walls, trying to scratch my way from this terrible truth. The truth I had killed my precious Courtney. I must have a screw loose upstairs. How else could a mother kill her own child? I should've died that day, not her. I was a terrible, terrible person. Isabella was not safe here. She was not safe around me.

I waited until I heard the shower running before I tiptoed past to Isabella's room. If she didn't want to talk about why she was here, I would find out for myself. I hated snooping, but Isabella had given me no other choice.

A ping of guilt tugged at me, but I pushed it aside. I unzipped her big duffle bag sitting on top of the bed and rummaged through it, trying not to leave anything out of place. The anxiety built as I kept looking over my shoulder, afraid she'd enter at any second.

All I saw were clothes, a few books, receipts, and a notebook at the bottom of the bag. I opened the closet door, looking over my shoulder. I couldn't tell if the water was still running or not. Nothing was in the closet except a few clothes hanging on hangers and a pair of shoes, boots, and sandals on the floor.

I surveyed the room, but it was devoid of anything out of place. Isabella's phone was plugged into a charger on the nightstand, a half empty bottle of water, a pair of earrings, and a book. Nothing suspicious.

Think. Think.

I got on my hand and knees, grunting—I wasn't a young duckling anymore. I scanned under the bed but saw nothing but a few cobwebs under the bedframe. What did I think I would find in here? A big flashing sign with a message? Some mysterious box with hidden secrets? I crept to the door and listened closely for running water. Isabella was still in the shower. *Good.*

I returned to her bag. I must be missing something. *The notebook.* I gently slid it out, as to not disturb anything. As I opened it, a few pieces of paper drifted to the floor. I bent as my knees cracked and popped to pick them up. Newspaper clippings. I read the headlines. *Double murder.* I flipped to the next one. *Husband and Wife Found Dead in Home.* And another, *Murder Victim's Daughter Missing.* I gasped. A picture of someone resembling Isabella but with longer and different colored hair stared back at me. I quickly scanned the article. *Trevor and Ashley Williams. Hammer. Slit throat.* My hands trembled. I quickly slid the clippings into the notebook and shoved it to the bottom of the bag and crept from Isabella's room before she could catch me in here.

I couldn't decide if Isabella was running from someone or if she had done something terribly bad. It felt like barbwire twisting and cutting my insides, my nerves on edge. I ventured into my bedroom, closed the door behind me and paced. How do I pry the truth from her without her being suspicious of me snooping in her things?

I couldn't deal with all this. My journal. Isabella. My head was swimming. This complicated *everything*! I must confront her. There was no other way around it. I would wait patiently in my room before I pounced on her like a tiger.

I waited and waited and waited. What was she doing in her room? She should've been out of there by now. I knocked on her door and patiently waited.

"Yes?" I heard faintly behind the closed door.

"Isabella?" I paused. "We need to talk."

"Okay. Just give me a minute."

"I'll be downstairs." I stared at the closed door, waiting for a response, but it never came, so I walked away.

Twenty minutes passed before she descended the stairs.

My stomach was summersaulting.

Isabella approached me.

"Please have a seat." I pointed to the chair opposite from me. I shifted nervously and cleared my throat. "I have a confession to make." I looked at my hands folded in my lap. After a few moments, I looked up; Isabella's expression was hard to read. "While you were in the shower, I went through your things."

Isabella gasped. "Why?"

"You won't tell me why you're here. You keep telling me you don't want to talk about it. You show up out of the blue, and your behavior has been very bizarre. I just wanted answers. It was driving me crazy. I had to know. I thought I would find the answers in your room." It came out rushed. I talked fast when I was nervous.

"And did you?"

"Did I what?"

"Find the answers?"

"Not really. I have lots of questions. I found the newspaper clippings."

A long awkward silence hung between us. I looked at Isabella, at my hands, then back at Isabella again.

"Oh. That." Isabella slouched and sighed heavily.

"Are you running from someone, or did you do something terrible?"

Isabella just stared ahead, not at me, not at anything.

My gaze dropped to the floor then at Isabella. Her silence made me nervous. "Look. If it makes you feel any better, I've done something terrible myself."

"You have?"

"I spent ten years in a mental institute for the criminally insane."

"What did you do?"

"I was diagnosed with postpartum depression and drowned my daughter in the bathtub."

Isabella gasped.

"I've spent all this time blaming my husband, turned him into a monster, because it was easier than dealing with the truth. I started believing the lies. And all the memories just slowly turned to dust and faded away. I have empty holes in my memory, but it's how I survived."

Isabella sat in silence for a moment, trying to digest everything. "I had a psychotic break. Delusions. Voices in my head. I had to do what they were telling me. I had to kill my father. He—he killed his wife and Mary to protect me."

My hand flew to my mouth, and I gasped.

"We never had a chance. We have bad blood. Our ancestor was one of the most notorious serial killers out there. We had no chance to live a normal life. It's not our fault. It's in our blood and running cold through our veins."

I shook my head in disbelief. "What are you talking about?"

"Jack the Ripper."

Everything rushed at me about the night Mary and Trevor had visited the nursing home—the curse. "But I broke the curse on this family when you were a just a kid."

"I don't know if there ever really was a curse. If that's the case, then why did all these horrible things keep happening after you had broken it?"

"I don't know." I shook my head.

"We have bad blood. That's why. We had no chance." Isabella hung her head.

"I need to get out of here. I need fresh air." I stood, grabbed my jacket hanging on the coat rack and stuffed my keys into the pocket. I closed the door behind me and beheld the freckled stars that twinkle against the faint moonlit sky. I released a deep sigh and lowered my head as I walked to my car. I sat for few moment, staring blankly. I put the car in Reverse and drove aimlessly through the deserted gravel roads. Destination: far away from here. I just needed to get out of the house that was destroying my mind and suffocating my soul.

I need fresh air.

I drove for a long time, lost in my thoughts. I looked away from the road for just a second then back again, panic rising as a dog stared back at me like a deer in headlights. I quickly turned the wheel, hitting the soft shoulder. I jerked the wheel in the opposite direction. I watched helplessly as my world turned upside down over and over again.

My body thrashed violently.

A loud crash erupted.

A crack echoed in my skull.

Warm liquid ran down my face.

I began swimming in a dark rabbit hole and then—

Nothing ...

AWAKE

I peeled open my eyes, shielding them from the bright light that streamed through the curtains. I raised my hand to my head; the pounding was horrendous. It was sore, and I winced in pain. I gasped as I traced my fingers along a rough line that ran along the left side of my skull, sending shivers through me. My head was fuzzy and full of empty holes.

What happened?

Confused, I scanned the room that was finally coming into focus. In the corner was a gray plush reclining chair frayed and threadbare, a small round table with two chairs, a small TV hanging on the wall, and a window hidden behind a faded curtain. A typical hospital room, bland and devoid of any charm. I sighed heavily.

What am I doing here? How long have I been here?

I had so many questions.

A light tap on the door startled me as someone pushed through the wide opening. "You're awake." The nurse smiled. She looked to be in her forties, petite, with dark short hair and glasses too big for her small face.

"What am I doing here?"

"You were in a car accident. Your vehicle rolled several times, and you were rushed in here by ambulance with fatal injuries."

I raised my hand to my head again, frowning.

"How are you feeling?"

"Sore and in a lot of pain." I winced.

"That's understandable. You'll be in pain for a while." The nurse lowered her head, not saying anything for a moment. "By the way, my name is Anne. I'll be your nurse for the next few hours." She checked my vitals, her touch making my skin jump. "Sorry about my cold hands. I have poor circulation."

The room fell silent for the next few minutes. Once she had finished poking and prodding me, Nurse Cold Hands spoke again. "The doctor will be in later to check on you." She smiled and walked out the door, closing it lightly until I heard the click.

Alone in the room, I panicked.

I can't remember anything! Not just what happened that led me here but everything! I don't even know my name!

My stomach clenched, and a large lump formed in my throat, making it hard to breathe. My eyes widened with fear as the realization hit me like a brick wall.

This can't be happening! I'm just stuck inside a cruel nightmare, and I'll awake from it soon, I repeatedly told myself. Saying it more would make it more believable.

My breath quickened, and my heart hammered. I felt dizzy and nauseated. I thought I would get sick. I sat upright abruptly, bracing myself.

What's my name? Why can't I remember my name? What day is it? What year is it? This is terrible! Wake up! Wake up! Wake up! I repeated as I slapped my face hard.

I brought my knees to my chest and rocked back and forth while tears welled in eyes. My stomach summersaulted as the nausea clawed at my throat. I made a beeline for the bathroom, clinging onto the wall for support. When I pushed through the door, I grasped on the sides of the sink, holding myself up. I looked in the mirror, but I didn't recognize the person staring back at me. My eyes were swollen; all the color was drained from my face while beads of sweat formed at the nape of my neck and hairline.

I felt *so* hot.

I didn't feel good.

I felt like I would fall over.

I lowered myself to the ground and crawled to the toilet as I heaved clear liquid into the sparkling-clean porcelain. It splashed back into my face. I got sick again. I slowly reached for the tissues on the toilet back as my hands trembled and wiped my face and mouth. I felt so tired. I curled up on the floor and closed my eyes.

***

"Ms. Walker? Ms. Walker?" the voice echoed in my head.

I groaned, peeling open my eyes as the room came into focus. I blinked hard, realizing I was lying on the bathroom floor. *What am I doing here?* I rolled over, slowly leaned up on my elbows and pushed myself off the floor. My head was foggy and full of clouds.

A light tap echoed from the door. "Mrs. Walker?"

I groaned again.

"Ms. Walker, let me help you up." The doctor walked behind me, grabbed me from underneath the arms and lifted me to my feet. "Let's get you to your bed where you can lie down." He lead me to the bed as I shuffled my feet. "There you go."

I sat on the edge and fell backward against the pillow in exhaustion.

"I'm Dr. Knutson, by the way. Nice to finally meet you, Angelina. How are you feeling?"

It took me a moment to speak. "Like shit."

My doctor was very handsome. He was tall, athletic build, pale blue eyes with crows' feet when he smiled. He was probably in his forties and had a dusting of salt and pepper in his dark hair. It looked like he had forgotten to shave this morning, but I liked it. Facial hair always looked nice on men.

"That's quite understandable. You've had quite the accident," the doctor replied while reading my chart from the clipboard.

"That's what the nurse told me."

"You don't remember?"

I shook my head vigorously.

"Head injuries can be complicated. You fractured your skull. Fortunately, someone saw your accident and called nine-one-one An ambulance was close by and got there quickly. We operated almost immediately, but you lost a lot of blood."

A whimper escaped my chapped lips. "Wh-what's my … name?"

"You don't remember?"

I shook my head, looking at my hands folded in my lap. I was embarrassed.

"Angelina Walker."

"Angelina?"

"That's right." The doctor nodded.

"How long have I been here?"

"Nine days. You were in a medicated coma while we monitored your brain swelling."

I touched my head and winced, shutting my eyes tight.

"Your head will hurt for the next few weeks. You were lucky. If someone hadn't heard the crash, you would've bled out, and you wouldn't be with us right now."

"I don't feel lucky." I moaned in pain.

"You need to get some solid food in your stomach. All the medication we have been pumping through you will make you feel queasy and lightheaded."

"I don't feel hungry. I just want to sleep."

"You've been sleeping for nine days. All you've had is an IV drip to keep you hydrated. You need to eat something. I'll have your nurse get you a menu."

"Okay," I whispered. "I'll try."

"Thank you. I'll check on you tomorrow. Hope you feel better." The doctor gave me a weak smile as left the room, shutting the door behind him.

My head swam with so many unanswered questions. I thought hard, trying to remember the slightest of anything. I stared blankly, my head pounding in my skull as my entire world vanished before me. I ran my fingers along the scar, a shiver coursing through me.

A knock on the door snapped me into reality.

A young, thin lady with short dark hair peaked her head around the door before entering. "Hi, Angel. I'm here to bring you home."

"Who are you?" I asked, confused.

"Isabella."

I shook my head.

"The doctor said you've lost your memory. I'm your sister's great-granddaughter. I came to stay with you for a while. I'm here to take you home." The stranger smiled.

"I'm sorry, but I don't know who you are."

"It's okay, Angel. I'll take good care of you."

EPILOGUE
JAKE

I was on my phone, not paying attention, and ran into Angelina outside a grocery store. I was more than embarrassed. I felt terrible. She had eggs in a bag, and they cracked and broke, making a horrible mess.

She was stunning—naturally beautiful, with long straight blond hair, tall, bright emerald-green eyes, and a flowing sundress. It was love at first sight. She was everything I was looking for—beautiful, intelligent, with a good sense of humor and personality, and a great cook. I couldn't ask for more. Before we got married, we were finishing each other's sentences. We were perfect for each other. But it was too good to be true.

I moved in with Angel a month after our messy collision at the grocery store. We definitely moved too fast, but it felt right at the time. I was completely smitten by her, head over heels in love. We got engaged six months later, got pregnant and married three short months after.

Angel was sick the first half of her pregnancy. She couldn't hold anything down. She was miserable.

I felt terrible for her. I sat next to her and held her hair when she got sick in the toilet. The pregnancy changed her. I had heard her hormones would change, but this was different.

She became very depressed. She would cry for no reason. Get angry with me for small things. She lost it one night.

I had forgotten to grab bread on my way home from work. The transformation right before my eyes scared me.

Her eyes went wild; her breathing sounded like an angry wild animal ready to attack. She went into our formal dining area, grabbed the plate she had dished up for me for dinner and threw it across the room. The plate shattered, and food slid down the wall.

I didn't know what to do or how to react. I stood frozen in shock.

She rushed at me and punched my chest, telling me I was useless. Then she broke down in tears, dropped to the floor and rocked back and forth in hysteria. Within five minutes, she went from being happy to see me to angry then crying hysterically.

One night, she snapped, came after me with a hammer.

I locked myself in the bedroom.

She put a hole through the door.

Through the closed door, I heard a loud thump. I came rushing out, afraid of what she had done; she was pregnant for god's sake.

She was curled in a ball on the floor, sucking her thumb like a baby.

Confused, I knelt next to her, rubbed her back and told her everything would be okay.

She sat up, hugged me so tight and cried into my shoulder. She sobbed through her words, having a hard time getting them out. She was hysterical, kept repeating how sorry she was and didn't know what was happening to her.

I suggested we see a therapist.

She nodded through her tears. She regarded me with such sadness and confusion in her eyes.

I ran my fingers through her hair, kissed her forehead and whispered, "I love you, Angel."

Her body trembled and shook.

I think she was afraid I would leave her.

***

The doctor diagnosed Angel with antepartum, also known as prenatal depression. She warned us that since she was already experiencing symptoms during pregnancy, she would more than likely have postpartum depression and that we needed to be prepared for even more drastic mood changes after the baby was born.

At first, Angel felt guilty and shameful for what she had been putting me through. But I knew this wasn't my Angel; it was the hormones causing these mood swings.

A month before her due date, things got really strange. She blamed me for things, twisting everything. She acted scared of me. Anytime I would try to hug or kiss her, she would flinch, and her body tensed. This upset me more than I can explain. I'd been so supportive through all her crazy mood swings. I attended every OB appointment with her and all her therapy sessions. Sometimes we'd visit together, and other times I'd sit in the waiting room, so Angel could speak to her doctor privately.

I had noticed over time that a big empty space grew larger between us. And soon that gap would never be mended again. The bridge we had built to fill this massive gap between us crumbled and crashed to the ground the night she killed our daughter.

I couldn't forgive her. I should've protected our daughter. I should've admitted her into a psych ward. But she seemed to be doing better. If I'd just listened to that nagging feeling at the back of my head and had admitted Angel when things had turned for the worst, Courtney would still be alive.

I miss her so much. I can't sleep or eat. I started to drink a lot to dull the pain. I slept with her teddy bear every night. I can still smell her on it. I can't remember the last time I fell asleep without crying—crying for our ruined marriage, my broken Angel, and now our dead daughter.

I know I should've left a note. I should've talked to Angel. But I was so angry with her. We had been sleeping in separate rooms for months now. We didn't talk. We just walked around like zombies. *I hated her.*

I packed my bags in middle of the night and never turned back. Every time I saw Angel, I was reminded of what she had done. I wanted so badly to put my hands around her neck and squeeze all the life from her, to make her pay for what she had done. Instead, I left.

No letter.

No call.

Nothing.

I heard the front door slam. I whipped around, and Angel was rushing down the porch steps at me, screaming at the top of her lungs, "You can't leave me! I've lost everyone I care about!"

"I can't do this, Angel. Please let me leave." I paused, noticing lights turning on inside neighbors' houses. "I don't have it in my heart to forgive you. You killed our daughter." I hung my head as tears fell in sheets.

Angel's eyes turned to glass—an evilness behind them, black and empty. She raised her arm. I saw the hammer gleam in the moonlight. And everything went black.

I could now live peacefully with my baby girl. Forever.

Made in the USA
Columbia, SC
23 October 2022

69823080R10117